Keach McKennie has been estranged from his dad ever since his 21st birthday. His dad promised him a hefty check but gave him a strange novel instead. Now, seven years later, Keach is dealing with a breakup and is cleaning out his home. He finds the book and soon learns there's an unopened birthday card in it.

Inside the card is a check for three hundred thousand dollars.

It should be the answer to all his worries, but he's too late to cash it. Foolishly, he tries anyway and finds the account his dad once owned has been flagged. LA's fraud squad claims Keach's dad was a bank robber.

When Lucas Warner, a sexy, but cynical cop launches an investigation, he is convinced Keach is involved in stolen bank funds . . .things take a disastrous turn.

Can Keach prove his innocence to the man he finds so attractive? Or should he get used to the idea of a future wearing stripes?

Reboot My Heart
Copyright © 2019 A.J. Llewellyn and D.J. Manly
ISBN: 978-1-4874-2698-9
Cover art by Martine Jardin

Published by eXtasy Books Inc or
Devine Destinies, an imprint of eXtasy Books Inc

Look for us online at:
www.eXtasybooks.com or www.devinedestinies.com

REBOOT MY HEART

BY

A.J. LLEWELLYN AND D.J. MANLY

DEDICATION

To anyone who ever dreamed of getting a windfall.

CHAPTER ONE

"Does it spark joy?" the shiny, delightful, elfin Marie Kondo asked the bemused-looking hulk of a man perched on the edge of his bed.

Keach watched, fascinated. He'd never seen a functional hoarder before. Or such disgusting surroundings from a man who loved *stuff* so much he had eight rooms full of multiple household objects, and seven closets bulging with clothes.

The man pawed through a huge pile of clothes he hadn't worn—by his own admission—for seventeen years. He scratched his head. "I dunno. Clothes are clothes."

And yet, the man hadn't thrown a single thing on the pile to be discarded or donated. Each item seemed to have such painful attachments, Keach would have burned them eons ago.

Marie Kondo clapped her hands and jumped up and down with glee. Her bouncy hair followed her movements. Evidently, she got a kick out of tough customers.

Keach McKennie had watched all eight episodes of her Netflix series *Tidying Up*, and so far, his efforts to thin out his possessions hadn't sparked much joy. In fact, he'd already developed rampant anxiety over things he regretted tossing out over the last few days. The end of his ten-year relationship wasn't just the end of an era. Keach was officially in a mental canoe on rocky seas, paddling to a destination unknown.

He glanced at the underpants drawer he'd dragged to the living room and peered at the contents. He'd Kondo-ed the heck out of his closet, but damned if he could muster a glint of anything joyful about underpants.

The man on the TV started crying. Marie perched like a pixie in front of him, her beautiful face creased with concern. Keach almost turned off the show. Tempted to re-watch the entire second season of *Killing Eve*, he manfully focused on the job at hand. Even though underpants were underpants. His sparked neither happy thoughts nor such utter anguish they reduced him to rubble. He plucked out a pair of boxers with the slogan *It Ain't Going to Suck Itself* emblazoned across them. *Holy heck! What are they still doing in here?* He tossed them to the floor.

Oh, there's a spark. Fury. I can't believe Joe left those here. He took my prized comic book collection – seventeen years of Dragon Ball Z! – but left me his garbage.

On TV, the weeping man was now rolling his underpants into colorful tubes he lined up in boxes, sliding them into his bedroom drawer. His smile was so wide Keach wondered if wacky tobacky or psychotropic meds might be involved.

Huh. Keach was bored now. He decided to toss the drawer's contents. Now he had no cookware, underpants, socks, or dress shirts. No dress pants. No suits. And he was down to two T-shirts, three pairs of jeans, two pairs of sneakers, and two pairs of flip flops.

What did I do? What the hell am I thinking? He gazed out of the window. Santa Monica was still there. The scent of the ocean soothed him, and from his vantage point, he could see the big Ferris wheel moving steadily around on Santa Monica pier.

He scrabbled over to the window and studied the hordes of people walking the foggy lengths sampling free eats all in the name of gay pride. Yup. It was Gay Pride Weekend, and Joe had left him for somebody he said needed moral support in coming out.

"He needs me," Joe had said when he bolted two days before.

Much of what he'd taken—including Keach's personal pride—seemed to fit into a compact U-Haul. It was only after Joe had left that Keach realized a lot of his own possessions had vanished with his lover. It seemed fitting to finish the job himself.

As Keach turned back to his near-empty living room, he realized he'd soon fill the spaces again. Only this time, he could do as he pleased. He could put anything he wanted in the apartment. No Joe to bitch and moan about feng shui and bad angles and unlucky designs.

We had the luckiest configurations according to him. And look where it got us.

He gazed at the two boxes of books he'd packed to donate to the library and sighed. He'd been meaning to take them there for days. They had a weekend sale, and he was sure they could use them.

Keach suddenly felt the need to get rid of them. And his underpants. He bagged up the latter and picked up one box, carting it to the garage. He'd come back for the second one. Ignoring the homeless man pawing through the recycle bin, Keach popped open the truck to his Prius, the only possession he was determined to keep. He stuffed the box on top of his multitude of recyclable shopping tote bags.

"Hey, Keach," the homeless man said.

Keach glanced at the man.

"Why did you start shredding paper?" the guy scowled. "Don't you know paper's not a valuable resource once it's shredded?"

Keach cocked his head, curious. "Paper's valuable to you? Why?"

"I'm a poet." The homeless man, whose name was Winter, pushed back the battered straw hat he always wore away from his sunburned forehead.

"A poet." *That explains a lot. No wonder he's homeless.* Keach sighed, chastising himself for his mean thoughts.

Until a few months ago, Winter had lived across the road on Nielsen Way, a piece of prized real estate in Santa Monica. Over the years, Winter had become a well-known eccentric to his neighbors, who either loved or hated him.

Keach had loved him until Winter's alcoholism had taken a toll on his health and personality. In fact, Keach had always assumed the man was homeless until he saw him stacking stuff he'd taken off the streets and shoved onto his balcony. Keach lived right across from him and watched with mounting dismay from his bedroom window as the collected junk filled the space. It turned out it was Winter's mom's apartment, and he'd cared for her until the day she died.

I still respect the heck outta the guy for caring for her as long as he did. I stopped talking to my parents years ago. He swallowed. Hard. With Adelaide's death, her social security had shriveled up, and Winter couldn't afford the rent. It was a situation that had alarmed Keach and other neighbors. Few people could really afford to live in Santa Monica, but Keach was lucky. His building was rent-controlled, and he'd lived there fifteen years in relative comfort. With Joe gone, he'd have to tighten the belt a bit, but he'd manage. He always did.

There but for the grace of God go I.

Winter's sister had put him up in a cheap rental in Hollywood, but Winter took the bus — three of them, actually — to Santa Monica each day. He pushed around a shopping cart and filled it with found treasures, sipping a bottle of Bulleit rye that rendered him unconscious by lunchtime. At that point, he'd nap, sprawled on his former lawn.

He'd once asked Keach what had happened to his valuables. He meant the junk he'd put out on the balcony. The landlord had it all hauled away. It had taken him weeks to clean out the apartment. Now the new tenant had no idea what a crummy dump it had been. It looked like every other white-paint-grey-carpet box, like all the others in the neighborhood.

Winter knew his stuff had been dumped but couldn't

accept reality. Eviction had come unusually fast for Winter, but the landlord had known the man had no means or mental stability to buy himself more time via the court system. Marie Kondo would have had her work cut out with this guy.

"I like to write," Winter said. "Shredded paper's no good. I can't write on that."

"I shred it because of identity theft." Keach knew that Winter had heard the story, but clearly just wanted to talk.

"But I want to write," Winter whined. "I *need* to write. My eyes aren't so good now, so reading's hard." He waved his arms around. "I had to give up on newspapers. The print's too small."

Keach could smell the booze on the man's breath now . . . and his unbelievable body odor. He reached into the book box in his trunk and withdrew a bizarre notebook and pen set Joe's mom had given him for his birthday. Keach had wondered about the gift's meaning but gave up looking for the hidden explanation and tossed it in the book box.

"Here," he told Winter, handing him the journal. "It's a bunch of different notebooks and a pretty nifty pen."

Winter scrunched his nose as he read the line stamped on all the pages. "You can never have too many shoes." He looked down at his mismatched, threadbare pair. "You know me so well."

Keach laughed. "How about a book? I know you love to read."

"I just told you I can't read so well now. Don't you listen?"

Not really. Speaking of bizarre gifts . . . the book on top had been the weirdest thing he'd ever been given. His dad had thought the memoirs of a country priest a fitting *gift* for Keach's twenty-first birthday. Keach had been livid when a messenger delivered the tome. It had been wrapped in gaudy silver paper, a birthday card atop the book. He hadn't even read the card. What kind of gift was that? Especially since his dad had told him, dozens of times over the years, that he would be given a huge chunk of money for his twenty-first birthday.

A book. That's what he got.

He'd called his dad and still remembered their horrible discussion.

"Did you open the card?" his father had asked.

"No! I don't care about the card. You promised me." That was fifteen years ago. He'd relied on the promised money. His dad had been a wealthy man but was stingy as hell with Keach. They hadn't spoken since, and Keach felt a pang of guilt that his dad had tried to communicate with him. Now the old geezer was dead. End of discussion.

"You've got a cruel sense of humor," Winter whispered.

Keach offered Winter a twenty-dollar bill. The man was weird about accepting cash. He preferred to recycle cans and bottles down at the supermarket. He called it his job. But he took the money. They both knew it would buy him a couple of bottles of rye.

"Thanks." Under his breath, Winter muttered, "Last of the big spenders." He pushed the hat forward over his brow once more. "I'll take the book, on second thoughts. I've got nothing better to do."

Keach handed it over and slammed the trunk closed. It was only as he'd driven halfway down the block that he remembered he'd forgotten to pack the second box of books.

He moseyed on over to the library on Santa Monica Boulevard and paused out front as an elderly man grabbed donations from the stream of vehicles ahead of him. Keach waited, and for a moment, the elderly man caught his gaze. *Geez. He looks like Dad.*

Keach rubbed his eyes and blinked. *No. He doesn't. What the hell is the matter with me?* He stared at his fingers, gripping the steering wheel so hard his knuckles were white. *It's the book. I haven't thought about it in years . . . until I decided to donate it.* He frowned. Maybe he could ask Winter for it back. *Heck. Maybe I should buy another copy. Dang. It's all I have left of Dad. Maybe I should have kept it.* He struggled with his thoughts. *No. It doesn't spark joy.* He concentrated on deep, relaxing breaths. They didn't help.

He inched forward as the elderly man emptied boxes and tote bags of books onto a library cart. When he reached the front of the line, the man held up a finger and wheeled the cart into the library. He soon sprinted back with an empty cart, and Keach turned off the ignition, popping open the trunk. The old man smiled at him and hauled out the box.

He worked so fast, and seemed so fit, Keach felt guilty that he wasn't doing more community work himself. He tried not to feel even more guilty about his job, working as a travel agent—and securing massive deposits from people who wanted to travel to space—for Fletcher Celestial, a new, multi-million-dollar rival for Richard Branson's Virgin Galactic.

"Thanks," the old man said, giving him a wave.

Keach waved back and got inside his car again. When it was safe to merge with oncoming traffic, he pulled out into the flow and almost got into an accident. That was beach driving for you. Sometimes he wondered where people got their licenses, because they drove so badly. He checked the time. Ten to twelve. He had forty minutes to make it to the Figtree Café in time for lunch with Bobby. Bobby was the best. He always showed up when Keach needed him.

He veered south, contemplating returning his car to his parking lot and walking to the boardwalk where Figtree was located. He had time. Keach turned the car around again and lost fifteen valuable minutes trying to get back home and ended up parking at a beach lot. Never mind. He'd probably need an afternoon nap after all the carbs he intended to consume over lunch, and having the car close by would be handy.

Keach squeezed the Prius between two 70s style VW vans filled with ganja-smoking teens. Now that weed was legal in California, life seemed to be a nonstop contact high. Keach parked, activated the alarm, and stepped over to the board-walk. As he passed the parade of goofy beach stalls, hawking everything from dubious souvenirs to psychic readings, he casually flipped through his cell phone until he came to Joe's Instagram page. He almost fell over. Three posts this morning after days of silence.

Walking with my beloved, read one caption. *Wilshire Boulevard, here we come*, was another.

Keach came to a dead stop in the middle of the boardwalk, almost colliding with a bicycle rider. Though it was illegal to ride on the strip of concrete meant for pedestrians, nobody followed the rules. Keach ignored the rider's expletives and moved to the soft safety of the sand. He couldn't believe what he was reading. Wilshire Boulevard had been their secret. For ten years he and Joe had walked from one end of Wilshire to the other in a single day, covering all fifteen point eight miles, stopping for coffee, kisses, then dinner in the evening. Then they'd take a taxi home.

Now the idiot was doing the walk with some other guy. His *beloved*. The third photo featured an actual photo of said *beloved*, who up until now had been a mystery man. Keach stared at the handsome, exotic-looking, long-haired husband thief.

Damn. He's hot. Boy, would I like to give him a one-way ticket to the moon. And I'm the guy that can organize it for him, too.

Keach read some of the comments. *Whoa!* There were a lot of question marks. One follower Keach recognized as a guy from the gym had written *Who dis?*

Joe had responded with *PM'd you.*

Keach closed his eyes. *And so it starts. Emptying my closets doesn't begin to deal with the issue of friends wanting to know what went wrong.* People would call Keach. Which side would their friends pick? Who sparked the most joy for them?

He hurried to Figtree, where Bobby was waiting for him. He'd snagged a table for two on the far outside wall, alone in a sea of noisy, chatting diners. Keach bumped into a couple of strollers and a surfboard, he was so fixated on reaching Bobby. A part of him wanted to go home and go back to bed. Another part wanted to talk. Bobby was scrutinizing his cell phone and glanced up, a guilty look on his face.

"Heya," Bobby said.

He'd just landed his dream job of running an Internet cosmetics empire. Keach tried not to stare. The very handsome Bobby Rymer must have been sampling the merchandise. Being his best friend, Keach knew Bobby's face well. There was an odd, puffy look to his mouth and eyelids.

"What did you do to yourself, Bobby?" Keach blurted.

Bobby rolled his eyes. "It's Robert now, babe. Why do you keep forgetting? It's our new version of Botox. You like?"

Yeah. If you dig looking like a tortured puffer fish. "Um, well, when the swelling goes down—"

"What swelling?" Bobby's fingers flew to his face. "Where?"

"Mouth and eyes." Keach regretted saying something now. He adored Bobby—Robert.

"Fuck. I've been icing my fucking face for days. My lips are so frozen I can't even smile without it hurting. Have you seen Joey's Instagram? Who the fuck is the long-haired git he's dating?"

"No idea." Keach was feeling terrible now.

"Since when did he start going for Euro trash?"

Keach laughed. He couldn't help it. *Beloved* was a hot-looking dude. For a home wrecker.

Keach's cell phone rang. It was his brother, Mike. They were barely on speaking terms now that both their parents had died. Mike had inherited a small fortune on *his* twenty-first birthday and used it to open a surfboard shop down in Huntington Beach. Now he ran six of them and held a surfing contest each year to benefit at-risk kids.

Keach ignored the text, even though Mike's words wounded him to the core.

When did you finally get rid of that lowlife?

Keach turned off the phone. He glanced at Robert, who was now peering at his face through the gleam of the flat side of his knife.

"Still puffy." Robert sighed and put down the knife. He glanced at Keach, a weird look in his eye. "I have a confession to make."

"Yeah. What's that?"

The waitress approached and greeted them. They knew Saskia well. "Hey, guys. The usual?"

Keach and Robert exchanged looks.

"We have to," Robert said. "You know that, right?"

"Yeah. We have to." Keach glanced at the waitress. "The usual. Thanks, Saskia."

"Awesome. Keach. How's my campaign going?"

"You're still in the lead." He smiled.

Saskia wanted to be the first waitress in space and had started an online petition through Keach's company web page. That had spurred other wait staff across America to start their own petitions, but Saskia was a strong contender. She appeared to be the only waitress in America who enjoyed her job and wasn't trying to become an actress, model, or something else. She also blogged about it. People who placed their cutlery incorrectly on their plates drove her nuts. So did people who took out their false teeth and cleaned them in their water glasses. She had another advantage of being blonde, blue-eyed, and drop-dead gorgeous. Just the way American men seemed to like their women.

"So." She pointed her pen at Robert. "It's the puffed pancake for you and"—she swung around to Keach—"the nuclear pancake for you."

"Right," Robert said.

"Coming up." Saskia took off, returning seconds later with two cups of coffee.

Robert was laughing at his own reflection in his knife again. "Would people laugh if I posed for a photo with my breakfast?"

"Not at all," Keach assured him. It struck him how odd and how apt their menu choices were. Robert had been the one who'd first picked out the nuclear pancake for Keach.

"You're selling space travel, and soon we'll all be ducking and diving from nuclear wars, and we're gonna be calling you," Robert often said. "Just warning you. I demand first-class seating, even in outer space."

Keach was now addicted to the nuclear pancake's combination of apple butter and organic maple syrup. Try as he might, he could never replicate the recipe at home. He was right to have tossed his cookware. *Maybe I should take a cooking course. I know! Paris. I could travel there and take lessons at Le Cordon Bleu. Or that hot new cooking class instructor I heard about. Whatshername? At Home with Patricia Wells. I bet she has dozens of pots and pans. Do they spark good feelings for her?*

Saskia sidled back over to them. "I forgot to mention that the puffed pancake's gonna take about a half hour. We're swamped today."

"Okay," Robert said, looking like it wasn't.

"I'll bring you a snack," she promised. "A chocolate waffle."

"Awesome." Robert sounded happier, but his face didn't move.

"Do you need ice?" Saskia looked worried.

"Yes. A thousand times yes. I left my pain meds at home."

Saskia took off again, and Robert picked up his knife once more, studying his facial damage.

"You said you had a confession to make," Keach reminded

him.

Robert glanced at him. "Man, do I have a big mouth. I wasn't . . . I shouldn't have said anything."

"Out with it."

"I told Joe I'd have dinner with him and Eduardo tonight." He winced, anticipating Keach's reaction.

"His name's Eduardo?"

Robert nodded, his expression miserable. He fidgeted with his knife, resisting the urge, it seemed, to use it as a mirror again. After a few moments of silence, he said, "Say something."

Keach looked off to the left, studying the array of expensive footwear the diners wore. The only one not wearing shoes was somebody's poodle, crouched under a chair. The poodle looked as happy as Keach felt. He took a deep breath. Then another.

Et tu, Brute? Keach had never felt so betrayed. His life was going to hell in a hand cart. He suddenly wondered why his brother had called him. It had cost his ego dearly to call Michael two weeks ago and casually ask if he was interested in flying into space.

Michael had said yes and ponied up the non-refundable quarter of a million-dollar deposit for the ticket. Keach had no doubt his brother had done it in the interest of expanding his celebrity profile. And also, Keach was certain, so he could tell everyone he knew that he'd helped his loser brother out by buying the ticket.

"Say something," Robert repeated.

Keach shrugged. He'd known Robert since kindergarten at the Country School in the Valley. They'd become instant best friends and had kept it together even after Robert had transferred out to Campbell Hall in sixth grade and Keach had been shunted deeper into the San Fernando Valley to the Lewis Carroll Academy of the Arts. He still had fond memories of the now-shuttered school, which only went to the eighth grade.

His thoughts turned to Michael, who'd been twelve years older than him, the product of their father's first marriage to an actress called Bella Boston. Michael McKennie, Sr., had a hard time talking about Bella, who'd given up everything to marry him. At least that's what Wikipedia said about her. She'd mysteriously disappeared, and although Keach had never met her, she more than resembled his own mom, Harper Collins, who married his dad a year after Bella vanished.

Keach was born a few months after their marriage, which shocked the Hollywood gossips at the time, and seemed to enrage Michael Jr.

Mike had spent his teenage years skulking in his bedroom, listening to heavy metal and experimenting with psychedelic drugs. He also became the first person their father knew who could score Dilaudid just walking down the street. Mike had been, in Michael Sr.'s words, *a horrible teen* who'd made a profitable business at high school from the age of fourteen selling Ketamine — a horse tranquilizer known as Special K — to his fellow students. When a bunch of teens were found pie-eyed, hanging from the school rooftops and perched hallucinating in trees, Mike had been suspended. He returned with a renewed vow to be smarter about his entrepreneurial ways and sold OxyContin, or hillbilly heroin, to his classmates.

This resulted in Mike being expelled. For his final year of high school, he was put in a lockdown facility in Minnesota, allowed home only for short vacation breaks. Each time he was aggressive and violent toward Keach, who tried his hardest to stay out of his way.

"He's a troubled soul," Keach's mom would say. "Just give him time."

By then, Keach, like Robert, was enrolled at Campbell Hall. Keach and Robert had been closer than brothers, and Michael, once he returned home full-time, resented it. He was chummy with Keach one week, then Robert the next. But Keach and Robert remained tight through high school graduation and college. They'd been friends, business partners, and had briefly flirted with the idea of sex, but knew it would kill their friendship. Their bond had been unbreakable.

Or so Keach had always thought. "Where are you meeting them for dinner?" He hoped his voice didn't reveal the brokenness he felt.

"Vespaio."

Keach nodded. It was one of the most expensive restaurants in downtown LA where Wilshire Boulevard ended. He and Joe had been there last year for their end-of-walk dinner. Now Eduardo would get to go. "Enjoy it," Keach said. His appetite had vanished. He took out his wallet and peeled off a couple of twenties, threw them on the table, took a swig of his coffee, and stood.

Robert's face turned ashen. "You're not leaving?"

"How long have you known about them?"

Robert had reached out a tentative hand to him but jerked it back. "A while," he admitted.

"How long is a while?" Keach admired his own calmness when he was feeling like Bruce Banner about to unleash the Hulk.

"Six months." Robert shrugged. "It's been hard not to tell you."

Keach almost laughed and leaned forward. "I recommend the fish stew tonight. It's really very good."

He turned on his heel and walked out, shocked to see Winter hovering outside the café. The hostess stood by him, holding one of Figtree's large, laminated menus in front of him as a sort of barricade.

"Hey," Winter said, his face looking more sunburned than ever. "They won't let me in, and I thought you should have this." He handed over an envelope. "It was inside the book. It has your name on it." Winter slid his straw hat back over his forehead and disappeared into the beach crowd swarming the boardwalk.

Keach held the envelope. He recognized it as the unopened birthday card his father had sent him with the book. He'd been so angry with his dad for so long he'd refused to read it, even though his father kept calling saying, "Just read it. Please."

Tears filled his eyes. He thought he'd thrown it out, but clearly, he hadn't. His father was still with him, even when Joe wasn't. Through brimming tears, some deep form of self-punishment kicked in and he opened it. He withdrew the blue and white Happy Twenty-first Birthday card and skimmed over the joyous sentiments.

May all your dreams and wishes come true.

Words swam. His father's handwriting. *So proud of you. Dream big.*

A tear fell on a folded piece of paper, hiding the rest of his words.

A check.

Oh, no.

He opened it and blinked. It was a check for three hundred thousand dollars. *Oh, man, it's more than he once said he'd give me. More than a quarter of a million dollars.*

That had been his gift. The *real* gift.

And he hadn't seen it.

Holy, heckin', cruddy, crap.

CHAPTER TWO

Too late now. People had to cash checks within six months in the US. And it had been fifteen years. *Fifteen!*

He swatted at his eyes, trying to stop the tears from blinding him. The check had been written on a Downey Savings & Loan account. Keach had never heard of it but was certain it no longer existed.

"What's going on?" Robert came up behind him and turned Keach around, gripping his shoulders. "Dude. Keach. Pull yourself together, man. What is it?"

Keach couldn't speak. Aware of passersby staring at him, he dropped his head and passed the card and check to Robert.

"Holy crap," Robert murmured after a few seconds. "Did you have any idea?"

"Of course not." Keach snatched back the check. "If I'd known, I'd be talking to you from my private island right now." He scanned the paper once more, folded it, and scrubbed at his tear-stained eyes with the backs of his hands. He opened the check again. Yep. There it was. A cool, crisp three hundred thousand dollars. Made out to him.

Only it was too late now.

"You think Michael knew?" Robert asked.

"Aw, crud. I have no idea. I didn't even think of that." Keach's tears had stopped flowing, but he needed to blow his nose.

"Come back to the table. You need to eat. And we need to figure things out." Robert gripped Keach's elbow and steered him back to the table. A busboy hovered, one of their dishes in his hand. He put it down when the waitress shooed him away while Robert plopped Keach back into his seat.

"He's had a shock." Robert's voice boomed over the noisy crowd.

Keach's head throbbed. He couldn't believe his bad luck. No. His crappy decision making. Over and over, his father's voice rang through his mind. *Please open the card. There's a surprise. Please listen to me.*

Why didn't I humor him? Why didn't I open it, then make a decision? I'm a rotten, stinkin' son. That's what I am.

"Do you want to call Mike and find out if he knew you had that big check waiting on you?" Robert asked.

"No. Because if he did, I will never forgive him for not telling me. I can't believe what an ass I've been."

Saskia swung by and placed glasses of iced water in front of them. She snatched up their coffee cups. "Let me get you hot coffee. Be right back." She moved off with her usual breakneck speed.

"I'm Googling Downey Savings & Loan," Robert muttered as Keach gulped at his water glass. "Damn. They closed back in 2008. That makes sense. Right when the real estate crash happened. All those mortgage loans defaulting." Robert looked up from his cell phone screen. "Do you know if your Dad lost his shirt, or was he okay?"

"I have no idea. I haven't spoken to him since . . ."

"When he wrote the check."

"Right."

"I knew that, but I always thought you'd talked and never told me." Robert shot him a curious glance.

"No. I never did."

"Do you think Harper knew?" Robert asked.

"No. I'm certain of it." Once again, his thoughts raced. *God. All those lunches with Mom, who was having problems of her own with him. It was always like that. When I was a kid, Harper would take me to Du-par's, ostensibly for a special meal of hamburgers and*

17

cherry pie. She would say how grown up I was and thought it was a compliment. I guess for her it was. She was always in a hurry for me to grow up so could confide in me and not have people tell her it was inappropriate. But it was. She didn't want to talk to me, but at me. Our mother-son meals were a ruse so she could rant about Dad.

She was such a good woman, and he was very hard on her. She'd always lived under the shadow of the enigma that was Bella Boston. Dad was as mercurial with her as he was with me. In fact, both Dad and Michael were. One day Dad loved her, the next he railed against her imagined crimes against him.

"If Mom had known there was any money to be had, she'd have told me." Keach tried not to think about her awful passing. She had moved in with him and Joe just before, and Keach could pinpoint the start of their romantic troubles to the few weeks he had been looking after her.

"Yeah. I don't doubt it. She would have told you, and he probably loved having one more secret against her." Robert's phone beeped. "Well, the good news is Downey was taken over by US Bank, and they're definitely still in business. There are branches everywhere, but with your dad gone, and now your mom, you might have trouble verifying the check was signed by him. You may want to ask Mike to vouch for you. He's a successful businessman. And he got a check too, didn't he?"

"Yeah. But years before me." Keach's spirits plummeted to his shoes. He dreaded having to involve Michael. His brother always seemed to be so competitive with him, and they'd never been close. He'd always been grateful for his friendship with Robert because he'd found the support and closeness he'd never had from his own family. "What I could have done with that money," he blurted.

Saskia returned with their coffees and Robert's puffed pancake. Keach barely noticed his own decadent concoction when Saskia placed it in front of him.

"Have something to eat," Robert urged before scrutinizing

their waitress. "You know, Saskia, you really should do something about your wrinkles —"

"Wrinkles?" She looked appalled. "I'm only twenty-three!"

"They're fine lines now," he said, apparently unaware she was on the verge of tears. "But in a couple of years, your face will look like a relief map of Switzerland. Here's my card."

It was a simple white thick square business card. A very impressive, hot new style, with *Robert Rymer* written in bold, black embossed lettering spread across the top.

"I'll give you a good discount if you call me directly."

She took it, but her sunny disposition had transformed into stormy weather as she turned on her heel and left them.

Keach would have rebuked Robert except for the fact he was in torment. He stared at a teenage couple kissing outside an ice cream stand. They seemed so happy and carefree. *Was I ever like that?*

He remembered his numerous calamities over the years. For one, his prized, classic 1974 Karmann Ghia he'd bought for three hundred bucks and restored painstakingly for a year. It had developed a host of issues he'd had no money to fix. Then he'd had to quit Northwestern, the college of his dreams, for Santa Monica Community College. *Ugh.* The list went on and on. With money, he could have done so much.

Robert forked the cascade of fruit atop his pancake. "I can't even open my mouth wide," he grumbled. "It hurts. Why the fuck did I do this to my face?"

It tickled Keach's funny bone. "Because you have the one thing I've always envied and always lacked."

"Oh, yeah? And what's that?"

"The vanity gene." Keach's thoughts moved to the host of personal items he'd discarded. *God help me. I have to replace it all now. That's gonna play havoc with my finances. Maybe it's not too late to cash the check.* He picked up his phone and called Michael. His brother's ridiculous message, which always started with *It's a great day in sunny LA!* went on for almost a full minute.

Keach left a voice mail. "Hey, it's me. Listen, I can't even believe it, but I just found the check Dad sent me for my twenty-first birthday. I never even knew I got it. Did you?" He caught Robert's incredulous stare. Keach was disgruntled. He knew his brother always had his phone clamped to his ear and had most likely declined to answer. "I don't know what to do. Don't know if I can cash it. Would you be willing to go to the bank with me and verify that it's genuine? Please. Get back to me. Thanks." He marked his message urgent and ended the call.

"You called him and put all your cards out there? Wow." Robert bit into a raspberry. "I bet he acts like a dick. Do you think he knew about the check?" he asked again.

"Something tells me yes." Keach took a tentative bite of his pancake. It was good and helped lift his mood. Maple syrup was his go-to food item. *Help. I threw out my only bottle of it. But then it was past the use-by date.*

"I think so too. Wonder if he'll call you back." Robert sipped his coffee.

Keach was startled. "You think he won't?"

"What's in it for him?"

"True." Keach's thoughts circled in his addled brain. When he got his money—and he was determined to do so—he would give Winter some cash. If the homeless man hadn't given him the card, he would never have known about his rotten luck. "Where are US Banks?" He picked up his cell phone to start searching.

Robert waved the idea off, fork in hand. "There's one right on Second Street. I checked. Corner of Santa Monica Boulevard, but I don't think you should go there without Michael. You're gonna need backup." Robert reached across the table and forked a piece of Keach's pancake. "It looks like up until a year or so ago some people were going into branches with their old Downey Savings & Loan bank books and were able to transfer funds to US Bank."

"Bank books. Wow. I don't think I've seen one of those for decades." Keach remembered his pride in opening his first savings account with money he'd earned as a tennis camp counselor. He'd opened and closed that thing over and over that summer, just admiring the handwritten entry for two-hundred dollars.

"I know, right?" Robert gave him a sympathetic smile. "You have to find some way to sweeten the deal with your brother."

"Yeah? How?"

Robert grinned. "He's desperate to date your friend, whatshername?"

Keach groaned. "Angelique?"

"Right!"

"Dude, I could never hate her that much."

Robert laughed. "I'll throw in some free cosmetics for her. She's an influencer. She'll love it." Robert punctuated the thought with his knife, which was now being put to proper use. "She and I could make a deal."

"I'm getting a headache with all these deals." Keach glanced at his phone, wondering how long it would take for Michael to return his call.

Brunch over, Keach drove Robert back to his apartment. Robert had keys to Keach's garage and had parked his vehicle in one of Keach's tandem spaces because he was too cheap to pay for parking on the beach.

"Besides," Robert had insisted, "I needed a good walk."

Robert lived in the east LA suburb of Silverlake but loved the beach life, so he came to Santa Monica whenever possible. He often parked in Keach's space but was usually good about moving toward the front so Keach could park behind him. This time somebody else had parked behind Robert. Keach didn't recognize the car, and by rights, he could have had the vehicle towed, but they decided to knock on doors to see who owned it.

He parked his own car in the fire lane and left a note on his dashboard with his cell phone number. He scrawled an explanation that somebody had parked in his space. The last thing he wanted was to get his own car towed.

They raced upstairs. An hour later, an apologetic woman moved her car out of the space, and Robert stopped by Keach's apartment for a bottle of water.

Keach was antsy. No call from Mike. He wanted to get to the bank before it closed. He *had* to cash that check.

"Jesus!" Robert gripped the front doorframe as they entered the apartment. "You've been ransacked!" His gaze swiveled everywhere. "Don't tell me Joe did this."

"Nah. I did it myself."

"Oh, God. You've been watching the queen of clean again." Robert helped himself to the fridge. "At least you didn't throw this out." He peered inside. "May as well have. It's empty."

"Yeah. Sorry about that."

"You okay?" Robert asked him, his tone gentle.

"Not really. I can't stay here. It feels weird. I'm going for a drive."

"Whatever you do, don't toss that box of books. It looks creepy in here. Like you can't afford a chair. What are your guests supposed to sit on by the way?"

"I don't know." Keach shrugged. "You're talking to a guy who's down to his last pair of underpants."

Robert cocked a brow in his direction. "How recently did you change them?"

Keach laughed. "I put 'em on today. I'll buy more. I threw almost everything out. I miss some of my shirts and pants already."

"I don't. You've had some of those things since college."

"So?"

"It drove Joe nuts."

Keach rolled his eyes. "Now you tell me."

"I'd go shopping with you, but I wanna hit the gym, then take a power nap before I meet up with Joe later." He slid a guilty glance Keach's way. "Are you gonna hate me forever if I go?"

"Nah. Just don't leave my life, okay?"

"I could never do that." Robert gave him a hug. "Can I give you some advice?"

"Sure."

"Don't sound too desperate with Mike. I know it's hard, and it's a boatload of money, but try and sugar up that deal, like I said."

Keach nodded, but as soon as he was back in his car alone, he knew he'd call his brother again. He followed Robert downstairs and got behind the wheel of the Prius. That was when he noticed that the building manager had left a note on the windshield.

He got out and grabbed it. *Phew*. It was a nasty reminder not to park in the fire lane. It only made Keach's mood even darker. He waited until Robert left and called Mike. His cell phone got good reception in spite of being fifty percent down on its battery charge. He went straight to voice mail and left Mike another message.

He pulled out into the street, wondering what to do next. The truth was, he had money in the bank—there was good income booking space travel. He'd also received a twenty-five-thousand-dollar bonus for booking a ticket. He could get used to bonuses like that. However, he wasn't sure he wanted to fly to the moon himself, even though staff members for Fletcher Celestial were invited to travel at reduced rates, once they sold over five million dollars in tickets. So far, he had one sale and two pending transactions. If they went through, that put him at seven-hundred-and-fifty thousand. He had a long way to go before he got to five big ones.

Keach figured since he now had a full stomach it would be a good time to go grocery shopping. It would stop him from buying junk like *Little Debbie* Swiss Rolls and pancake batter. That would be useless when he didn't have a frying pan. He sighed. Since Joe's defection, he'd been making one stupid decision after another.

The prospect of replacing his lost household items wasn't as daunting as he'd first thought. He'd start small and wouldn't have to confer with anybody. He could buy what he wanted. He headed over to the Third Street Mall and bought a bunch of stuff at Bob's Market, including pancake batter, eggs, butter, milk, syrup, bottled water, apples, *Little Debbie* Moon Cakes *and* Swiss Rolls—because he couldn't resist—and even a frying pan.

With these items stowed inside his trunk in insulated tote bags he bought at the store, he headed to Marshalls at the Westside Shopping Center and loaded up on socks, underpants, shoes, shirts, trousers, and jeans. He picked up a discounted toaster oven he found in the clearance aisle of the home goods section. He wondered if the toaster oven was safe, since it was only ten bucks, then decided he'd risk it.

He spotted a stack of cookbooks and remembering he'd just unloaded some, he pushed his cart past them, his attention on gym wear. *Man, I'd gotten all my T-shirts nice and comfy. I'd broken 'em in. Did they really make Joe go nuts? Why didn't he ever say anything?*

As he stood in the long line for the registers, he contemplated his purchases. He'd grabbed a ton of stuff he needed but wondered if he'd regret them. He took a deep breath. For two days he'd been off his game at work and knew he had to get back to pestering people on his endless supply of call sheets.

Wanna fly to another galaxy, far, far away? had become his joke phrase when he contacted the rich and/or famous. They usually laughed and indulged his sales pitch.

One woman had said, "Oh, no. I can't forget that episode of *The Twilight Zone*."

He knew the episode she meant, and frankly, it freaked the hell out of him, too. A race of aliens visited the earth to take earthlings on an all-expenses-paid trip to outer space. Some of them carried a book called *To Serve Man*, and as eager humans boarded the spaceships, a government official warned them — too late — "It's a cookbook!"

I think I'll stay here and stick with pancakes and moon pies.

Back in his car, he was proud of his new belongings loitering with intent in his trunk. But still, he didn't want to go home. Being a Prius owner, he was thrilled that he rarely had to buy gas. Six months he'd had it, and the needle had hardly moved from the full position. He plugged his cell phone into the USB port to charge it, then drove and drove, heading east, turning up the radio when Lauren Daigle's haunting song *You Say* came on.

He forced back the emotions so close to the surface. The song spoke of all the things he felt. *Will I ever get over losing Joe? Was I ever important to him?* He got on the 405 freeway heading north, wondering why he was even doing this. He waited until the song finished to call his brother again. The call rang through his dashboard radio. He still got Mike's voice mail, but this time he didn't leave a message.

As he dovetailed to the 101, heading to Hollywood, he found some of the lanes closed and took the Laurel Canyon exit to take surface streets. Up ahead on the right was a US Bank. Not keeping an eye on the traffic, he barreled into the bank's parking lot, earning a honk from the car behind him. He held up his hand in apology, making brief eye contact with the driver through the rearview mirror.

He eyed the tall, muscular, dark-haired man. *Oh, he's hot.*

He seemed too big for such a small car. It was a jet black shiny Camaro. Keach continued on his way and found a parking space near the bank's entrance. Inside, he approached a teller.

She smiled. She was quite exotic-looking with long dark hair and a dazzling smile. *She's beautiful. Why couldn't I be straight? She's just my type. Or would be.* His thoughts flashed back to the driver who'd honked him. *Now. He was my type.* He mentally slapped himself. *What the hell is wrong with me? I'm fighting for my life here!*

"Can I help you?" the teller asked, her smile fading a little.

"Hi. I know this is unorthodox, but I have a check from a long time ago my father wrote to me." He fumbled for it, pulling it out of the card, which he'd put back in the envelope. "He wrote it a long time ago," he repeated. When he handed over the check, the teller, whose name tag said Ariana, took it in her well-manicured fingertips and gazed at it.

Her apricot-painted nails matched her outfit. He wondered, idly, what she did with her nails when she wore a different color.

"You're right. It *was* a long time ago. We still get the occasional Downey Savings & Loan customer." She glanced up at him. "Very occasionally," she added, it seemed, for emphasis. "We don't cash checks beyond a hundred and eighty days and not for this amount. Can you have your father contact us?"

"He's dead."

Her lips formed into an apricot-tinted O.

"He gave it to me for my birthday. In this card. I was just ah, tidying up, and I found it." He passed the card beneath the thick wedge of bulletproof glass. She picked it up after a moment. It was as though she didn't want to touch it. She took the card out, read it, and pursed her lips.

"What about your mom? Can she verify the check?"

"She's dead, Jim," he said, using an old joke from the original *Star Trek* series. It didn't fly well with Miss Apricot. She stared at him, looking stunned. "I have a brother who also got a check from my dad—"

"Did he cash it?"

"More than twenty years ago."

"Hmm." She swung her gaze to her computer and tapped away on it with the tip of a pen. She glanced at him, a look of surprise on her face.

"What is it?" he asked.

"Nothing." Her lie was obvious. She shook her head and typed some more. "Um, sir. Could you please take a seat? I need to talk to the branch manager."

"Sure." He nodded. Maybe this was a good sign. Maybe there was some notification to make funds available should Keach ever pull his head out of his ass and try and cash it.

He moved over to a bank of hard leather seats and took one, watching the teller's progress toward a locked door. She knocked, and a woman came out. They spoke, then both of them glanced over at him. He smiled back, trying not to look or feel stressed out.

The second woman went back into her office. A few minutes later, cell phone in hand, she cracked the door open and poked her head out, clamping her gaze on Keach. When their gazes met, she retreated once again, and Ariana, who was still standing there, turned and glanced at him as well.

None of this worried him. He couldn't expect to bring in a very outdated check and to walk out with cash within seconds. He waited.

And waited.

And waited some more.

Thirty minutes passed, and the woman from behind the door came out and spoke to Ariana, who beckoned Keach over to her. She moved back to her window, and he followed her on his side of the counter.

She looked nervous. "We need to hang onto the check. Oh,

and the card. They're researching it."

Alarm bells rang in his head. "But I want the card. I'd like the check back, too, please. I need to call my brother. Once I can get him to come down here and verify —"

She looked a little panicked. She gestured for a male manager, who came to her, and they moved away from Keach.

Oh, no. Something's wrong. They're frowning. Holy heck. What have I done? His cell phone rang, and he became aware of a presence. It was the guy who'd honked him earlier. Keach noticed the man's frank stare and his unbelievably sexy presence. His phone call went to voicemail, and relieved to see it was Mike, he called him back. Ariana and the man she'd been talking to disappeared behind the door the other woman had vanished into.

Keach's cell phone rang again. Mike. He took the call, staring at the man who eased himself into one of the leather chairs in the middle of the floor. As Keach suspected, he was tall, muscular, and a beautiful mix of ethnicities. He wore jeans and a shirt over it, boots, and a leather jacket.

Looks like he works out regularly. God. And I just bought all those baked goods. Black hair, brown eyes. Handsome, but imposing. His gaze was so intense Keach felt intimidated yet drawn to the man and his close beard. *I wanna reach out and touch it.*

Mr. Handsome was staring at him. Suddenly he reached inside his jacket and took out a cell phone.

Keach suddenly remembered his own was ringing. He answered.

"Jesus Christ," Mike said. "Where the hell are you?"

"At the bank."

"Jesus Christ!" Mike shouted. "Are you fucking crazy? Why'd you go in there?" He let out a yell. "Get out of there, you fool. I had Dad's old account attached to mine and had an electronic alert placed on it. I've had three in the last two minutes after fifteen years of silence." A pause. "Don't tell me you tried to cash that fucking check."

"Of course I did. I've never had that much money in my life."

"Get out. Get out now. Walk slowly and keep talking to me. We're both about to get into a shitload of trouble. Come on. Move!"

Keach glanced behind the counter, but Ariana was gone. Mr. Handsome crossed the floor and was talking to one of the mortgage brokers at the entrance to one of the myriad glass-fronted business suites. Keach moved slowly but with rising panic toward the bank exit.

"Hurry," Mike urged. "Why the fuck didn't you wait to hear from me?"

"I called you several times. I thought you were messing with me."

"I was in dental surgery, numbnuts. Are you outside?"

"Yeah. I'm at my car. And don't call me that."

"Get in. I'll meet you—"

"Going somewhere?" a voice asked.

Keach turned. It was Mr. Handsome.

"Hi," Mr. Handsome said, flashing badge.

"Hi . . . you." Keach wasn't usually so openly flirtatious with strange men, but this one had piqued his interest.

Mr. Handsome appeared to be working hard to stop himself from laughing. "My name is Lucas Warner—"

"Oh. From the movie family? Are you a Warner brother?"

"Ah, no." He was holding a badge.

Keach swallowed. The guy was a cop.

"I'm a sergeant in the Hollywood Division Bunco Squad." He was holding a badge.

Keach swallowed. The guy was a cop. *No. Maybe he's an actor playing a cop.* "Get outta here! There's an actual Bunco Squad? I thought that was something straight out of old episodes of *Dragnet.*"

Lucas Warner frowned. "I'm with the Complex Financial Crimes Division."

Keach was fresh out of poor wit. He was fresh out of anything useful to say.

"I investigate fraud," Mr. Handsome, er, Lucas Warner said, a huge grin on his face.

Ouch. Keach gulped. "Fraud?"

"Yes, sir." He waited a beat. "You're not under arrest. Yet."

"Yet?" *Holy cow. Does that I will be soon? Oh, Mike. What the hell is going on?* As if Mike had read his thoughts, Keach's brother was yelling at him through the cell phone.

"Is that your brother, Mike McKennie?"

"Yeah. How'd you know that?"

"We've been watching him. Tell him to meet us at the Wilshire division in thirty minutes."

"Shit!" Mike screeched through the cell phone.

"Can I drive myself there?" Keach asked the cop.

"Sure. Just don't try anything cute."

"I'm not the cute type."

"I might argue with that," Warner murmured. He leaned closer. "You're gonna have to persuade me that you're not involved in this fraud your brother and father got messed up in." He snapped his fingers. "Maybe you know where the money is."

"What money?"

"From the bank robbery."

"I know nothing about a bank robbery."

"Come on, Keach. You know all about it. Your dad earmarked some of it for you. Although why you waited so long to get it is beyond me." His eyes glittered with anger. "See you at the station."

CHAPTER THREE

When he stopped at the intersection, Lucas glanced in the rearview mirror. *Okay, he's following me.* He was almost disappointed. He could have done with a bit of a challenge. He'd expected Keach McKennie to turn off and make a run for it. Seemed he wasn't going to.

White-collar fuckin' crime. The time he'd wasted building cases against these clowns, only to have them do less than a year in a lockup that was more comfortable than some hotels he'd stayed in, ticked him off. But this one was a whole lot of different. From the moment the file had been placed on his desk, he knew this was more than just a case of fraud. A little bit of digging around, and black and white burst into color. He was actually excited about where this might lead.

The light had changed to green. Lucas laid on the horn. He sincerely wished people would learn how to drive. He'd missed the light because some idiot was busy yelling into his cell phone. The traffic was building. It was going to take longer than he would have liked to get to the office.

Lucas checked his watch. *A quarter after four.* This day was one he'd intended to put in his *forget about it* box, but now, he wasn't so sure anymore.

He'd woken up hungover after coming home from an underground gay bar where the word *limit* didn't seem to be in anyone's vocabulary. Sam had been after him to check out this place for like forever. And Lucas had consistently responded with, "Not interested. These guys are into pain and role-playing and dressing up like bikers. It's not my trip."

But he'd gotten into yet another scrap with his former lieutenant the day before. The aftermath had driven home the fact that he was never going back to Homicide. He was condemned to work in the Bunco squad for time immortal.

"You can come back any time, Lucas," Hunter Brand had told him in his condescending little *I'm-a-real-bastard* voice.

Lucas had felt like punching him in his smug Lieutenant face.

"Don't blame this on me. I'm ready to forgive and forget." That smug smile was still plastered to Brand's face.

Lucas shook his head. "Well, I'm not. As long as you're still with Homicide, I'm staying far away. You said you'd transfer out. You gave me your word. That's why I dropped the whole thing."

"No, I said if I was proven guilty, I'd transfer out." Hunter lifted his head, then lowered his voice. "I'm not the one running around with all their sexual peculiarities hanging out for everyone to see."

"One day, some other officer is going to accuse you of sexual harassment, and you're going to go down." Lucas pointed at him. "You're safe for now."

Those words seemed to float right over Hunter Brand's inflated head. He came around to stand in front of Lucas. "We miss you in Homicide. You were the best damn detective on the squad. Too bad your personal life is such a mess. If I was ever desperate enough that I had to imagine someone coming onto me, I'd seek therapy. Personally, I think after that hot firefighter of yours died in that fire, you lost all professional integrity, Lucas."

Lucas clenched the steering wheel. He'd almost let Brand have it then. If he had, he'd be on suspension instead of dealing with the first potentially interesting case that had graced his desk in a while. He couldn't count how many times he'd thought of giving up, leaving this job, doing something else, but what?

The traffic had come to a stand-still, as if someone had pressed pause in the middle of a movie. Lucas rubbed his eyes and sighed, glancing again in the rearview mirror to see if his suspect had made a run for it. Too many cars. He couldn't see anything beyond a courier truck.

His cell phone rang. "Warner," he said, rubbing his jaw.

"Hey, catch you at a bad time, stud?" It was his friend, Sam. "You're not wrapping a tie around some white-collar executive, are you?" Sam laughed at his own nonsense.

"Yeah, that's exactly what I'm doing." He put him on speakerphone.

"So, how did you feel this morning?"

"The same way I feel now, like shit. Do you know I wasn't alone when I woke up this morning?"

"Woo hoo, good for you."

"No, not good for me. It was that guy who kept following me around all night."

"Oh, God." Sam burst into laughter. "You mean the little fella that wore the harness and kept saying he was a wood nymph?"

"Yeah, that be the one."

"So, he wore you down, did he? Was he good?"

"Get real! I found him sleeping in my shower. I almost stepped on his head."

Sam was still laughing. "Oh, my God."

"Complete with that leather harness get-up, and don't ask me what he had stuck in his ass, but I think he's gonna need heavy machinery to get it out."

"So, did you do him?" Sam was trying to reign in the laughter.

"Fuck off."

"How did you get rid of him?"

"I had to make him breakfast."

"You burn toast. I almost feel sorry for him."

"Um. Anyway, he ate standing up because of . . . So, how did he end up at my place anyway?" Lucas asked.

"Who knows. You took a taxi, right? He probably shared it, then just followed you inside. You were wasted. So, should we go back there tonight?"

"I'll pass. I'm working late. Got this last-minute interrogation to take care of. Don't know how long it will take. And I'm stuck in traffic."

"Is he cute?"

"Who cute?" Lucas inched forward a little. Some kid in the back seat of the car in front was sticking his tongue out at him.

"The suspect?"

"Ah, yeah, I guess." He took out his badge and held it up in the windshield. The kid disappeared from view.

"Bring him with you."

"Ah, no." Lucas moved through the light, spotted an opening and roared forward. "I don't date suspects, and I don't even know if he's gay. And even if he was, I don't think that place would be a good pick."

"Lucas, check the mirror sometimes. You are one of the hottest guys I know. If he's not gay, you could convert him. Make him confess everything."

"You're an idiot. I'm hanging up now."

"I love you. Kisses." Sam made big smacking sounds.

Lucas rolled his eyes and disconnected.

He and Sam had gone to high school together. They'd both come out of the closet around the same time and, of course, that meant they had to deal with homophobic bullshit. But Sam was half Lucas's size and not what one would call *butch* by any means. He got the shit beat out of him a few times. Lucas became his bodyguard, and the brother neither one ever had. They helped each other through all the rough patches.

When Lucas met Christopher, his husband, it was love at first sight. Lucas was fresh out of the academy, still in uniform. He'd been on the scene of a major apartment house fire, and there was this gorgeous firefighter, standing right in front of him. They were together almost two years then decided to get married. They spent a wonderful honeymoon in Jamaica. They were shopping for a house. A few weeks after they came back, Lucas was made detective. Christopher promised to be at the ceremony, but he never made it. A major forest fire broke out in Northern California, obliterating over eighty percent of the homes and killing ten people, including two firefighters, one of whom was Christopher.

One moment Lucas was receiving his detective's shield, proud and happy, and the next, his entire world came crashing to the ground. If Sam hadn't been around, Lucas would have sunk so far down in despair, he would have never been able to get up again. But Lucas had gotten up and hardened his heart. "Sam," he'd confided, "I can't ever go through that much pain again. No more."

Sam tried to tell him that one day he'd love again. It was the last thing Lucas wanted. As a result, he'd become far too promiscuous, not wanting to sleep with anyone more than once. His life had become Homicide. He lived and breathed it, and it was the only thing that propelled him out of bed in the morning.

Then Hunter Brand had transferred in from Phoenix, replacing his superior, Leo Murdock, who had taken early retirement. At first, it was great. Then it wasn't. Some silly flirting turned into some serious harassment. And Brand had been relentless, threatening Lucas's job, suddenly taking him off cases and putting him on other ones, to punish Lucas for rejecting his advances. Sam told Lucas to report what was going on, but he'd felt uncomfortable doing that. In the end, he'd had no choice, and the department sided with Brand.

"Lucas," they told him, "you've never hidden your sexuality. Hunter Brand is a married man, a church goer, three children. Are you sure you haven't misinterpreted these incidents?"

Sure, he'd misinterpreted Hunter Brand pressing him up against the wall in the bathroom and grabbing his cock. Or the time they'd gone together on a stakeout, and Hunter had unzipped his pants and suggested that Lucas blow him. Brand had told Lucas in no uncertain terms, sleep with me, or I'll make your life hell.

So the department suggested Lucas transfer, and the only place for him was on the Bunco Squad. So, here he was, day in, day out, dealing with conniving little fucks who liked to screw little old ladies out of their nest eggs.

The traffic had cleared now, and Lucas roared down Venice Boulevard. He was still driving Christopher's Camaro. This car was his baby, and after he died, Lucas didn't have the heart to sell it.

A few minutes later, he was turning into his parking space at the Wilshire Division. He sat there a minute, expecting to see Keach McKennie's car drive up. After a few minutes, he got out and walked into the precinct.

Monty was on today at the desk. He came from the same neighborhood Lucas had grown up in.

"Monty," he said. "How's it going? You got anything else for me?"

"Hey, Lucas, I should have something more for you later."

"Thanks," Lucas said.

Monty was a twenty-year veteran with a bum leg. He'd been shot on the job and was confined to the desk. Monty's elderly mother still lived in Ladera Heights, the same neighborhood as Lucas's mother, and they were both staunch members of the Ward African Methodist Episcopal Church. Lucas brought Sam there when he was a teen, and he was the only white boy in the room. It was funny to watch him clap and sway. Lucas's father, an Irishman, never attended church with Lucas's mother but then he labeled himself a *recovering Catholic*. Lucas, too, was a non-believer but whenever he visited his mother on weekends, he'd take her to church. She was so proud of him, telling everyone he was a police officer. Christopher used to go with them sometimes before he died.

Lucas's father had been a cop too. Retired now, he spent most of his time playing cards with the retirement club and driving his mother around when she did charity work.

He and Monty discussed their mothers for a few minutes. Monty's mom had been in the hospital and was now recovering at home.

Monty gave him a smile. "Your mother is there almost every day, bringing her books. You know how that woman likes those romance books. Your mom is a saint."

She was at that. Not easy to be married to a cop. His dad could work hard and play hard, but they loved each other and gave their only child a great home. His father had had a hard time with Lucas's coming out, but he was used to going against the current, marrying a woman of color. It didn't take him long to accept it, even walking Lucas and Christopher down the aisle at the wedding. His dad had loved Christopher.

Lucas glanced at the front door. "I'm waiting for someone, two people actually. Brothers." He took out his notebook and scanned the names. "Keach and Mike McKennie," he reminded Monty. "Give me a shout when they get here?"

"Sure thing," Monty told him, putting a pencil behind his ear. "Having a barbeque on the weekend. Why don't you drop by?"

"I'll try," Lucas promised. "Haven't seen my parents in a while."

"Invite them along."

"Okay," Lucas said and pressed the code, buzzing himself into the squad room.

His desk was near the back, and it was piled with crap. Great. He was not the best at keeping his reports up to date. He took a seat, looked through the new file on his desk. After a few minutes, he checked his watch. A quarter to six. Shit. He was starving. He buzzed Monty. "Anything for me?"

"Ah, someone just came in. Young fellow, fair hair? Looks petrified."

"That's him. I'm coming." *Finally.*

Keach McKennie was standing in front of Monty when Lucas walked out. He motioned to him. "Mr. McKennie?"

"Ah, yes, hello," he said, walking toward him.

"Where's your brother?" Lucas raised an eyebrow.

"I don't know. Isn't he here? I told him to come."

"No, he's not here. Follow me," he said, holding open the door.

"What's this about?" McKennie asked, practically walking on Lucas's heels. "I didn't do anything wrong."

"Have a seat," Lucas told him, lowering himself into his chair. He looked at him. "You want something, coffee?"

McKennie shook his head. "No. Thanks."

"What took you so long to get here? I've been waiting for almost an hour."

"I stopped for stomach acid stuff. Coffee will make it worse. I can't drink coffee after noon."

Lucas raised an eyebrow. "Thanks for telling me that."

"Well, I'm stressed out, so I could end up saying a lot of stuff you don't care about. What's going on?"

Lucas glanced at what he'd scrawled on his notepad today. "You believe in Martians?"

"Martians? No."

"Are you sure?" Lucas hid a smile. "Says here you sell tickets to Mars."

"Ah, yes, but" — Keach McKennie shook his head — "Fletcher Celestial is a legitimate enterprise."

"Huh. Has your boss, Richard Branson ever been to Mars?"

Keach gave a wan grin. "He's not my boss. He's my boss's rival. And no. Not yet. George Fletcher was working for Virgin when they financed two astronauts who went into space, the first launch from American soil since the last Space Shuttle in 2011."

"Huh. So he hasn't gone up there himself."

Keach McKennie just looked at him. He seemed petrified. "Richard Branson did. VSS Unity reached about fifty-four miles. He plans to go . . ."

"But you're making a living selling tickets to outer space."

"Yes."

"Do you think there's life on other planets?

"I don't know for sure, but I think so. What do you think?"

"Well, frankly, Mr. McKennie, if this is part of your sales pitch, I decline to comment. I think there are enough weirdoes on this one." Lucas held his gaze.

Keach had green eyes. They were bright and large. Nice. Everything he was feeling seemed reflected in those eyes. He said nothing, just stared. Damn, it was a disarming trick. It made Lucas want to respond. "So, you're selling the concept of alien life as the new thing."

"It's not new," Keach said. "It's a legitimate thing, what I do. It's not illegal. One day people will get to go to Mars. But right now, they'll settle for the moon."

"I'm not here to judge how you make a living. I want to know about this check you tried to cash today."

"I gave a book to a homeless guy. I know him pretty well and, anyway, it was a book my father gave me years ago. I was pissed about that present, so I never opened it. Winter gave me the check."

"Winter?"

"The homeless guy. He came to where I was having lunch—"

"How did he know you were there?"

"I'm always there. Anyway, that's all I can tell you, Detective, ah . . ."

"Warner."

"Right, sorry." Keach twitched a smile.

Lucas sighed. "Okay, so, let me try to decode what you just said." Lucas rubbed his head. It was going to be a long night. "You gave what book to a homeless guy?"

"The book my father gave me for my twenty-first birthday."

"Okay, why?"

"My father promised me some money, but all I got was a book. I never opened it. Then Winter gave me the envelope he found in the book."

Lucas just looked at him.

"It's the truth."

Lucas nodded. "It's too weird not to be the truth. So, you got the check, and you tried to cash it at the bank."

"Stupid, eh?"

"Well, it was a lot of money. And what about your brother? He seems quite well off. And I couldn't find an actual occupation for him. A few investments—"

"That's strange. He owns a chain of surfboard and sporting goods stores."

"So he actually works in them?" Before the man could respond, he asked, "Does he sell tickets to Mars too?"

"No," Keach replied. "But I just sold him a ticket. He invests in things. Dad gave him money when he turned twenty-one."

"And from the looks of it, he gave you some, too."

"I was not the favorite child."

"Okay. Why not?"

"I'm gay."

"Oh." Lucas nodded. "So, Daddy had a problem with your sexuality. All fathers do. They get over it."

Keach's eyes widened. "You're gay?"

"Mr. McKennie. Can we focus, please? My sexuality is irrelevant here."

"Sorry, it's just that, well, you are so . . . I don't know." Keach looked embarrassed. "Sorry."

Lucas sat back and folded his arms. "What?"

"Okay, so we are both gay, both have Daddy issues."

"I don't have Daddy issues," Lucas countered. "Let's talk about your father. He died in, ah . . ." —he checked his notebook—"two thousand twelve?"

"Yes."

"Did you attend his funeral?"

"No."

"Did you know your father had a criminal record?"

"Yes, he got in with some bad people before he met my mother. He never did time."

"Not true. He got a reduced sentenced because he turned state's evidence. After that, he worked as a mechanic."

"Yes."

"What about your mother?"

"She stayed with him because she was too afraid to leave."

"What about his first wife?"

Keach blinked. "She disappeared before I was born."

"And your dad didn't wait too long to marry her." He studied Keach's face to see his reaction.

"They fell in love. He wanted a mom for Mike."

"And your dad never talked about her?" He paused. "Bella Boston, I mean."

Keach didn't seem ruffled by the subject of one of Hollywood's most enduring mysteries.

"Not much. He and my brother were devastated. Mike

never really took to my mom, even though she tried so hard to be good to him."

"Has your dad ever tried to look for Bella?"

"Yes. In fact—"

"In fact, what?"

"Mike took a gap year after high school graduation and spent the time looking for her. Over the years, people have posted sightings of her online. Some of them contacted my dad. He and Mike followed up on every last lead."

That was news to Lucas. "And obviously they never found her."

"No." Keach lapsed into a troubled-looking silence.

"What? Lucas probed.

"Nothing. I just think it made Mike more depressed and angrier than he'd already been."

"You think she's alive or dead?"

Keach seemed to consider the question. "My mom and I talked about it a lot. She lived under Bella's shadow but always felt she was dead. She didn't think Bella would willingly stay away from Mike, or honestly, her small sliver of fame."

Lucas shut the notebook. He decided not to comment on that. Instead, he handed Keach the office landline phone. "Call your brother. Tell him if he doesn't come in willingly, I'm coming to get him. And he doesn't really want that."

Keach bit his bottom lip. He took the phone and dialed, his hand shaking. Lucas watched him. Keach McKennie waited for at least three minutes.

Lucas told him to hang up. "Where would he go?"

Keach shrugged. "I . . . I'm not sure." He handed the receiver to Lucas.

Lucas leaned across the desk. "Listen to me. I think he and your father were involved in a major bank robbery a few years before your father died. They got away with millions of dollars. Either you've kept your head in the sand all this time, or you're involved as well."

"I didn't rob any bank," he said, shaking his head. "I'm not close to Mike, and I was estranged from my Dad for years."

"Keach," Lucas said, "I believe you. But you need to tell me where to find your brother."

He sighed. "I could probably take you there."

"Take me where?" Lucas asked.

"Mike has a summer house."

"The one in Lake Tahoe."

"You know about that house?"

"Yes," Lucas said. He knew a lot of things.

"He might have gone there."

"Or, he's headed to Mexico." Lucas ran a hand through his hair and stood.

"I don't think so. I bet he's gone to Tahoe. He has friends there, and other places in Nevada. He told me something about Reno and Vegas. Investments."

"He's got seven vehicles registered in his name. Including a couple of Teslas in his company holdings. Guess he can afford a ticket to the moon." He noticed Keach's wince and went on. "There's four hundred and fifty miles between Vegas and Tahoe. Vegas is closer, but we'll start with Tahoe since you say he has a house there." Lucas picked up his cell phone.

"What are you doing?" Keach asked.

"I'm putting an all-points bulletin out on your brother and alerting the police in South Lake Tahoe. Since it's on the border with Nevada, I'll have them alert alpine patrols, too."

"No, please," Keach jumped to his feet. "Don't. Let me go and see if I can bring him back. Give me twenty-four hours."

Lucas put down the phone and glared at him.

"Please . . . please, Detective," Keach pleaded. "Let me do this."

It was against his better judgment, but there was

something in Keach's eyes. And there was a lot more he needed to know. This might give him the time to find out. "It's an eight-hour drive."

"I know." Keach met his gaze.

"Why do this?" Lucas asked him, curious about his motives. "You said you weren't close."

"I made mistakes with my father, and no matter what he did, he was still my father. I don't want to make the same mistakes with Mike. Now that Joe has left me, Mike is all I have."

"Joe?"

"Oh, sorry, I didn't mean to say that. Never mind. So, look, please, give me twenty-four hours to talk him into coming back."

"Fine." Lucas grabbed his car keys. "But I'm coming with you."

Keach's eyes widened. "Really?"

"Damn right. You think I'm going to run the risk of losing both of you? We'll take your car. Let's go." On the way out, Lucas stopped to talk to Monty. Keach waited by the door. "Let me know when the search is completed for Marianne Foster-McKennie. Call me."

"Why do I get the feeling, Lucas, you are not following protocol?" Monty grinned.

Lucas just smiled.

Outside, Lucas followed Keach to his car. The night was cool, and he could see a star or two. "I'm starving," he announced. "Let's get some food."

"Okay," Keach said, getting behind the wheel. "Where do you want to go?"

Lucas got in and adjusted the seat to accommodate his long legs. "Drive through is okay. I want to get going. I'll settle for a hamburger."

"I'll need to make a phone call to work," Keach said. "Take a sick day."

"Fine."

Keach drove out of the lot, then glanced at him. "This is part of your job, isn't it?"

Lucas turned on his phone and looked up. "Yes, and no. Set your GPS. And when you find a place for a burger, turn in."

Keach was quiet until they got to the burger drive-in. They sat eating without talking. Lucas was thinking about the robbery. It was probably one of the most professional jobs ever done, but they'd taken more than the money. Two people had died, one a bank teller, and another, an off-duty police officer who'd tried to stop them. The perpetrators had worn masks. Two men with automatic weapons. There was a getaway car with a driver waiting outside. There had been no leads until now, and if Keach McKennie hadn't decided to cash that check, there still wouldn't be.

When the food was gone, they were on their way. It was a long stretch of highway and not all that scenic, especially at night. The mountain road was dark, and thanks to California's energy conservancy, the streetlights were minimal. They gave off a strange, useless amber glow that had Keach hunched over the steering wheel, peering into the darkness ahead.

Keach was a cautious driver, and he didn't seem to be in any hurry. Lucas didn't blame him. He was probably worried about what he'd find.

"How can you be so sure that your brother is in Tahoe?"

"I just know. It's where he goes when he's—"

"He's what, in trouble?" Lucas glanced at him.

"No, sad. Mike suffers from depression. He was hospitalized once. He told me that when he feels the world closing in, he goes to the house in Lake Tahoe."

"And where do you go when the world closes in?" Lucas asked.

Keach glanced at him. "That's a personal question. How would you like it if I asked you that?"

"Go ahead. We got nothing else to do for the next seven to eight hours." Lucas sat back in the seat.

"Bare our souls?" Keach laughed. "Does it spark joy?"

"Does it do what?" Lucas wrinkled his brow.

"Spark joy? Comes from the *Tidying Up* series, you know, Marie Kondo?"

"Never heard of her."

"Seriously?"

"No shit."

Keach laughed.

"What's so funny?"

"You. You're funny."

"Okay, thanks I guess," he replied.

"I started watching her when Joe left me. I needed to declutter my life."

"I see. Now you want to talk about Joe?"

"Doesn't matter. He left me for a guy called Eduardo."

"Sorry. Ouch."

"Yeah, what about you? You don't seem the relationship type. Love 'em and leave 'em, a guy who looks like you?"

"Can we change the subject?" He didn't want to talk about the lack of love in his life.

Lucas looked out the window. It was dark now and not too much to see beyond glimpses of tall pines lining the highway. It was the first time he'd taken this route north. "I remember being on a road trip with my parents when I was a kid," Lucas said. "We drove east on Route sixty-six, LA to Vegas. We stopped at Red Rock Canyon, went camping along the way."

"That must have been fun."

"Yeah, it was, except for that time in this diner." Lucas remembered it like it was yesterday. "The owner didn't approve of bi-racial relationships. He said *The man and boy can stay but not the woman. We don't serve . . .* Well, he used the N word. He didn't want people of color in his establishment."

"Oh my God." Keach looked at him. "What did you do?"

"My mother had to stop my father from punching the guy in the nose." Lucas laughed. "We left and went somewhere else, but I never forgot that."

Keach reached over and touched his hand.

Lucas glanced down at Keach's hand on his, surprised.

Keach removed it.

He had no idea why he'd told this guy that story. Maybe it was driving up the lonely 88 highway. It was like reliving his childhood. His Irish grandfather had never approved of his father marrying an African-American woman. Lucas's father told him to go to hell one day when Grandpa Warner said, "Thank the good Lord, Lucas looks like a white boy."

Lucas's eyes were closing. Keach had to be tired, too. Lucas checked his watch. It was after eleven. They'd been driving just over four hours. "You can't drive all night. You should pull over, and I'll take the wheel."

"Or, we could stop somewhere, get a room. I'd pay." Keach sounded breathless when he said that. Then before Lucas could say anything, Keach said, "Oh God. Did that sound as if I was . . . I wasn't, you know, not really. It's just that, I feel bad. It's Friday night, and you're here with me, I don't even know if you'll get paid. You're doing me a favor and—"

"Keach!" Lucas interrupted. "Calm down. I didn't take it wrong."

"I mean, you must be used to being hit on, and I wasn't really. I—"

Lucas started to laugh.

"What?" Keach glanced at him.

"And you say I'm funny? Look, I think you're exhausted. Let me drive for a while. I'm used to long shifts."

"You sure?" He was pulling over.

They both got out at the same time, meeting in front of the car. Keach McKennie paused, looked up at him. "How tall are you, anyway?"

"Six-five."

"Wow, I feel like a kid standing here." He walked around and got into the passenger side. "We're going to need gas since I haven't filled up for a while and I only get fourteen miles with an electric charge."

"How do you like hybrids?" Lucas asked as he sat behind the steering wheel and adjusted the seat.

"Saves me money in the long run."

"Pricy vehicles." Lucas hit the gas, and they were rolling again.

"I didn't steal it, if that's what you think," Keach protested.

Lucas chuckled. "I didn't assume that."

"Ah, Detective, could you slow down, please. You're going way too fast."

"And you drive way too slow. So, why don't you close those big green eyes of yours and sleep?"

"How do you know what color my eyes are?" Keach poked him.

"I'm a cop. We notice things."

"And your eyes are brown, deep, rich pools of chocolate, large, expressive, even if you are cynical as hell." Keach was fiddling with the air conditioning. "Hot in here."

Lucas frowned. It was time to move out of this flirty territory.

"Come on, ask me why I know you're a cynic?" Keach probed.

"Don't think I will."

"Why not? Sometimes other people can see things you can't," Keach proclaimed.

"Not a big stretch, cops are naturally cynical."

"About love?"

"At the risk of sounding cliché, what's love got to do with it? You don't even know me."

"True, but I suspect that if you weren't here with me, you'd be finding someone to spend the night with."

Lucas glanced over at him. "And what about you and this Joe guy, who has left you for some Spanish dancer? Are you cynical about love?" Lucas held his gaze for a second then looked away. What in hell was this? It felt like they were the only two men in the world. It was mysterious and silent on that road and felt like it was the end of the earth.

For a while, Lucas thought Keach wasn't going to answer. Then suddenly he did. "When Joe left me, I felt as if I wasn't worth anything anymore. My whole world was him. I didn't know who I was without him. I don't expect a guy like you to understand that."

Oh, he understood more than Keach McKennie could ever know. He swallowed and listened to him talk.

"His scent was everywhere, on the sheets, the pillows. As much as I washed them, I still imagined I could smell him. I saw him everywhere. I dreamed about touching him and fucking him. But he was gone, and he wasn't coming back. He was shagging some other guy." Keach sighed. "I still don't know what I did to drive him away. Now this. My father didn't hate me after all. He sent me money, but I . . ." He stopped. "Detective?"

"Yeah?" Lucas's throat ached. Christopher's clothes were still hanging in his closet, but he couldn't bear to give them away.

"Do you think I'm a bank robber?"

"No," he said.

Keach reached over and squeezed his arm. "Thanks. I'm going to try to get Mike again." He put his cell phone to his ear.

Lucas knew Michael wouldn't pick up.

"No luck," Keach said. "I know he's gone to that house. Sometimes the signal isn't good. He keeps stuff there. I guess I shouldn't tell you, but that's the least of his worries. He said he hid some money from the IRS. Tax stuff. I didn't say that, okay?"

"I'm not the tax man," Lucas said. "I couldn't care less. Why don't you sleep?"

"Can't."

"Okay, tell me about your mother."

"My mother?" His voice shook a bit. "Why would I want to talk about her?"

"Was she happy with your dad?"

He felt Keach's gaze on his face. "For a time, I guess."

"When did things change?"

"I don't know." Keach scowled at the windshield.

"What did your dad tell you about Bella Boston?"

"Back to that, are we?" It seemed like minutes ticked by before he said, "Both and he and my brother say they woke up one morning and she was gone." There was profound sadness in his voice. "Mike said she didn't want to be with them. That's all." Keach cleared his voice.

"I see," Lucas replied. Another piece of the puzzle. "Did they see her leave?"

"No. Like I said, she just left."

"You said your brother tried to find her. What about your father?" Lucas glanced at him. "Did he look for her?"

"Secretly, he did. My father was bitter, I think. He wouldn't talk about her. She hadn't contacted any of her family. Why are you asking me all this?"

"Can you hand me my phone on the dash?" Lucas reached out for it and turned it on. There was a text message. He read it and closed the phone. "The house in Lake Tahoe, it was your father's before he died. He transferred it into your brother's name. Did you know that?"

"No. I didn't know that," Keach said. "The first time I saw the place was three years ago. My brother invited me and Joe to spend a few days with him. He told me he bought it."

"That's not true." Lucas pursed his lips. He wasn't quite sure how to tell Keach what he'd discovered. Lucas was used to going on hunches. He was truly sorry about how this one was playing out.

They were coming up to the exit for Tragedy Spring. How ironic, considering the subject matter. Lucas slowed when he saw the sign for the next town, Kirkwood, which boasted stick-figure drawings for gas and food. He signaled, veering off the highway.

"We're turning off?" Keach asked.

"Yeah. Let's see if we can get some coffee. I need to refuel."

"Do you think there's anything open at this time of night? It's nearly twelve-thirty."

"Let's find out," Lucas said. His years as a homicide detective had honed his instincts for this kind of a thing. This was getting more and more complicated. They came across Kirkwood Station, but all hope of a hot cup of coffee, and possibly a warm meal, were dashed. The building, which looked like a Swiss chalet, was locked, but the gas pumps seemed to be working.

"Thank God for credit cards. This is on your dime, right?" Lucas asked.

"Yeah." Keach got out and pumped the gas. "Damned expensive, but we are in the middle of nowhere."

"You're right about that. It smells good though, dunnit? All pine trees and . . ." He sniffed. "Do I smell chocolate?"

"Yeah. I have some in the trunk. I went shopping before my world fell apart." Keach shook off the gas nozzle and replaced it. With a sigh, he waited for the receipt, but none came. He took a photo of the readout on the pump. He moved over to the trunk, popped it open, handed Lucas a bottle of water and broke open boxes of *Little Debbie* cakes.

"Food of the gods," Lucas muttered, grabbing three packages of the chocolate cream rolls. He tore into one of them, glancing at all the other stuff in the trunk. "Were you headin' outta town? You've even got socks and undies in here." He gave Keach an accusatory glance.

"No. I did that Marie Kondo thing like I told you. I tossed out everything. I had to buy basic things."

Lucas poked around the bags. "Well, you're ready for anything. That's for sure. That frying pan you got there is making me really hungry. Thanks for the rolls. They're good. But snail larvae would have tasted wonderful right now."

"Yuck." Keach laughed.

Lucas's cell phone rang as he bit into his second roll. He checked the screen but said nothing, however, and they resumed eating and drinking in silence, leaning against the car.

"Detective?" Keach said. "What's going on? Why are you so quiet? What did you find out? You looked at your phone and got weird."

Lucas grimaced. Better to get it over with now. "Keach, listen. I've found out quite a few things recently. There was a body found buried near the house in Lake Tahoe your father owned."

"When?"

"It was discovered a couple of years ago. Long after Michael's mother disappeared. A forensic pathologist said the bones had only recently been buried there. Decomp, er, decomposition, happened elsewhere. She said the female victim was young, and she remains unidentified, but the cops at the time suspected it was Bella Boston—"

"Whaat?" Keach's eyes widened. "Why would she have been . . ." His voice faltered.

"Your father bought the house a few months before Bella went missing. I suspect she might have known about the robbery and—"

"The robbery happened *after* she died."

"No. There was another one. An earlier one. You said you knew he had a criminal record."

"Yes. He did about a year for fraud over a false report of a vehicle theft and robbery. He went down for that. I don't have any clue about another robbery. Except the bank thing you keep mentioning." He stared at Lucas, looking wounded. "Are you sure about this body?"

"As sure as I can be. It might never have been found except your brother sold the house and the new owners' dog dug up the body. Like I said, it's been a couple of years. They've tried to get your brother to pony up some DNA and he refuses. They can't legally force him."

"Oh, man." Keach shook his head. "It doesn't make sense. Surely he'd want the mystery solved once and for all. You have no idea what it's been like, being us. Even when we were children, kids would befriend us because their parents wanted to know about Bella Boston. As adults, it continues. It hurts my brother more than me because she was his actual mother. To me, she's just somebody that—"

Lucas pounced on his words. "That what?"

Keach shrugged. "Seemed to be the silent, shadowy third person in my parents' bed. My mom used to cry about her. She felt she could never compete with Bella Boston."

Lucas squeezed his shoulder. "You have some bad timing, my friend. I caught this case a month ago. I didn't want it, but there was activity—"

"What activity?"

"I'm not at liberty to say right now, but it's not looking good for your dad, or your brother."

Keach gaped at him. "Are you suggesting my father murdered Mike's mom?"

Lucas tried to formulate an answer, but Keach took off,

walking down the road like a zombie.

"Shit." Lucas chased after him.

Chapter Four

The Alpine lake region at night during the summer was still warm, but for some reason, it felt chilly as Lucas ran to catch up to Keach on the highway. "This is pretty dangerous, you know, walking out here at night."

Keach stopped walking. "There are people living out here. It's not exactly deserted." He was breathing hard, but he seemed a little calmer now. "What, you afraid to be attacked by a lizard?"

Lucas folded his arms across his chest. "Ever seen *Deliverance*? I can hear the banjoes in my mind." When Keach didn't respond, Lucas went on. "More worried about you being run over by a car, actually."

"There are no cars," Keach muttered, turning and walking back toward the vehicle.

Lucas remained quiet, falling in step beside him. "I'm sorry. I know that must have been hard to swallow. I gave it to you as easy as I could."

"Is that what you say to the guys you fuck?" Keach stopped and glared at him.

"Ah, no," Lucas replied. "Most of them don't want it that easy."

"You" — Keach jabbed at him — "set me up. You played me." He started walking again, this time, a little faster.

"Not quite," Lucas replied, following him. "I didn't know for sure about your mother, I mean Bella, until I got the message. I suspected."

Keach turned and glared. "If you're that good, what in hell

are you doing investigating bad checks? Shouldn't you be chasing Jack the Ripper, or something?"

"I did do that," Lucas replied, playing with the car keys in his hand. "I did that a lot."

Keach wore a bemused frown when they reached the car. He narrowed his eyes. "Are you fraud, or homicide?"

"At the moment," he said, getting into the car at the same time as Keach, "a little of both."

Lucas started the vehicle and pulled back out onto the road. "We will need to stop, I guess, get some sleep, a few hours."

"We're not that far from Tahoe. Maybe an hour."

"Yeah, but we need to get some rest, then ambush your brother when we have some backup in the morning. Driving around his place this time of night might alert him that he's being watched. I want to make sure he's there first."

Keach was quiet. He didn't say anything until they took the turnoff for Lake Tahoe Boulevard. "My life has become a nightmare."

Lucas nodded. "I know. Do you think Mike knows that your dad killed Bella?"

"No. You already asked me that. I mean, he still calls her Mom." He paused. "I know he misses her, and you haven't mentioned proof that my dad bumped her off. He was devastated over her disappearance." Keach shook his head. "My dad was married to my mom, and I was a little kid when I first realized that my family had a troubled past. I can't believe this is the first time I'm hearing about a body at the lake house."

Keach squirmed in his seat. "You know what it's like for Mike? She's a kind of Sharon Tate. Beautiful, blonde, mythical. Missing. If he had any idea she was dead, he wouldn't have gone looking for her. Would he?" Keach was looking at him for an answer.

Lucas didn't want to tell him he suspected Mike knew, might have even been involved. Instead he shrugged. "I'm not sure yet. Let's find a room." Lucas pulled into the first motel he found and sprinted to the front office, leaving Keach in the car.

A big sign behind the counter had handwritten gold-glittered words. *Happy 50th Anniversary Bob and Joanne.* There was a photo at the bottom of the sign of a grinning elderly couple. Bob looked just like the man behind the counter. Even down to the crooked glasses.

"You got a room with two beds, Bob?" Lucas asked.

"You and the Mrs. having a fight?"

"I'm with my cousin," Lucas lied.

"Got a queen. Two boys can share. Bed is plenty big," Bob insisted, passing Lucas the guest book after he'd photocopied his driver's license.

Lucas signed and paid cash for the night. As Bob counted the bills, Lucas flipped through the book. Looked like it had been here for fifty years itself. He stopped turning pages when Bob looked up at him.

"You gave me a dollar extra. I'll hang onto it for incidentals." Bob licked his thumb and painstakingly wrote out two cash receipts. When he smiled, his tongue and lips had gold glitter on them. In fact, there was a thin film of the stuff everywhere.

"You seem happy, Bob." Lucas smiled. "Happy Anniversary."

"Thanks." Bob gave him another glittery smile. "As I always say, life's short. Smile while you have teeth."

Lucas laughed and took the key cards and receipts outside. It was nearly one when he and Keach finally got into the room.

"So I've been thinking. How come they didn't do DNA tests on the body by the lake?" Keach asked.

Lucas was weary, and he had glitter on his hands and shoes. *I hate glitter.* "They did DNA, but they still don't know if it's Bella Boston. Apparently, she was adopted, and there's no next of kin except your brother."

"I didn't know she was adopted." Keach stared at him. "Why didn't they test Michael?"

"Like I said, he wouldn't give them DNA. They did some tests recently. Somehow, they got his DNA. All I know is, the results were inconclusive."

Keach stood rigid near the door, his gaze shifting from Lucas to the bed. "What does that mean?"

"I'm not sure. They've tried periodically to get Mike to come back in for more testing. As you know, there've been great strides in forensics since Bella vanished. They can't force him to submit with no concrete proof."

The words hung between them.

"The woman was found buried with a rag doll in her arms. Know anything about that?" Lucas asked.

"I wasn't even born when Bella vanished!"

"I know, I know. I just thought maybe you might have been told if she ever owned one."

"No. I have no idea. Everything I know about her I read in the media. There are dozens of websites devoted to her. Never heard about a doll from any of them, and my dad never talked about her. In spite of your bad impression of him, he never got over losing her. It really ate him up." Keach looked pissed. "And now, what, we share a bed?"

Lucas looked over at him and took off his jacket. "Don't get excited. I had no choice. I'll sleep in the chair."

"Is there a shower?" Keach walked over to the bathroom. "Yes," he said to himself, "I could use a hot shower."

"Go ahead," Lucas said, taking out his phone.

Keach disappeared into the bathroom. A few minutes later, Lucas heard the shower running. He checked the air conditioner. It was clunking away, but not cooling the stuffy room very much. "Shit." He took off his shirt and put it over the chair. Then he sat down and pulled off his boots. He was examining his handcuffs when Keach came out with a towel wrapped around him. Lucas glanced up, then away. Why was it the sight of a nearly naked man always stiffened his dick, whether it made sense or not?

"You're not seriously thinking of using those on me, are you?" Keach demanded, pointing at the handcuffs.

Lucas cut a glance at Keach, the water running down his chest and over his shoulders. He was slim but well put together, and the towel wasn't hiding much, especially the tent between his thighs. "Maybe you'd like it," he said, meeting his gaze.

Keach looked away and cleared his throat.

"You seem to have a" —his gaze went to Keach's groin— "problem."

The tip of Keach's penis was peeking out of the towel opening.

"Oh, shit," he said, rearranging the towel around him. "My underwear, well, I decided to rinse . . ." He stopped.

Lucas laughed. "With all the underwear you have in the car?"

"You're enjoying this?" He seemed outraged.

"A little bit." Lucas smirked. "Listen, I can't risk you taking off or alerting your brother so" —he got up and held up the cuffs— "maybe just one."

"Mister Goddamn Compassionate." Keach put his hands on his hips. "Where exactly am I going to go in the middle of the night?"

"You could take your car keys, your phone."

Keach walked up to him. "If you're going to use those handcuffs, Detective, you make sure as hell I'm going to enjoy it." Keach put his hand on Lucas's chest.

Lucas locked his gaze to Keach's eyes.

"You must find it easy to get people to confess." Keach met his gaze without turning away. "I got nothing left to lose. I could go to jail. I have no boyfriend, no real home. A few new household items. Nothing, really. And you're a cop breaking all the rules, aren't you?"

Lucas's pulse sped up a little. "It's hot in here."

Keach nodded. He unwound the towel and let it fall to the carpet. "You don't need those pants." Keach reached for the snap on Lucas's jeans. He undid it and unzipped the zipper, then looked up at him again. "Tell me to stop."

Lucas moved closer. "Why in the fuck would I tell you to do that?"

Keach pulled the jeans down over his hips. Lucas stepped out of them. As he did, Keach slipped his hands up over his chest, and Lucas bent his head to press his lips to Keach's throat. Keach lifted his face, seeking his mouth. Lucas hadn't truly kissed another man since Christopher, not on the lips. He froze.

Keach looked at him. "What is it?" he asked, sliding his hand down inside Lucas's briefs.

"I don't kiss on the mouth." As he said it, a profound sense of sadness came over him.

Keach put his hands on either side of Lucas's face. "Want to tell me why?"

"No," he said, taking a condom out of the pocket of his jacket. "What I want to do is fuck you." And with that, he picked Keach up, swung him over his shoulder, and dropped him onto the bed. He took off his underwear as Keach watched.

"You can use the cuffs if you want," Keach murmured, reaching for him.

Lucas shook his head as Keach pulled him down into his arms. "Doesn't look like I'm going to need them."

Whether it was right or wrong didn't concern Lucas. When it came to sex, he took what he wanted when he wanted it. Suspects weren't usually included in that kind of spontaneity. But Keach was sweet, like sugar candy, and he had an innocence about him that was particularly appealing. The way Keach was touching him set him on fire, and his impatient cock couldn't wait anymore to bury itself inside Keach delightfully round, tight little ass.

Once inside him, he wasn't sure who was moaning the loudest. As they fucked, Lucas found himself revising his definition of Keach. Innocence was only the outer layer. Keach was insatiable. He wanted more and more, and he wanted it rough and hard. Covered in sweat, their bodies moved against each other in an exquisite fiction that couldn't be denied. They fucked twice, then slept, and as the sun came up, Keach woke him again with lips, tongue, and fingers everywhere.

"Fuck me," Keach urged, "again," his demand punctuated by sliding a condom onto Lucas's newly awakened cock. "You are so damn beautiful. Ha! I wish Joe could see me now. He'd be eating his heart out. He'd forget that little jerk's name if he saw you."

"Maybe you should send him a picture," Lucas drawled, moving up behind Keach in the bed and yanking him up to his knees.

Keach looked back at him, breathing hard as Lucas moved his hands over his nipples and then pumped Keach's leaking hard-on. "You mean it?"

"Sure. I don't care. I'll even pose for you after, but we won't show all my face, okay?"

Keach chuckled, then grunted as Lucas pushed the head of his cock up inside him. "You ready?"

"Shit, yeah!" Keach cried out.

"Beg for it." Lucas grabbed an ear lobe with his teeth.

"Baby, please, deeper. Deeper. Yes!"

Lucas pushed Keach's neck down, pressing his forehead to the mattress. Keach's cries of pleasure filled the room. Lucas gave it all he could, adding his fingers to work Keach's cock and balls, making sure he and Keach came almost at the same time.

When his orgasmic bliss receded, Lucas pulled out and fell back on the pillow. "Damn. That was good. That was so good."

Keach crawled up beside him. He smiled at him, balanced on one elbow. "You're good at that."

He returned the smile. "Lots of practice."

"You gonna tell me why a gorgeous guy who fucks the way you do is alone?" Keach moved his fingers over Lucas's bicep, then he paused. "I didn't notice the tattoo. Who is he?"

Lucas had *Christopher* tattooed on his bicep right after they got married. Christopher had Lucas's name on his as well.

"You still love this guy?" Keach searched his face.

"I'll always love him," Lucas replied.

"Oh." Keach swallowed. "I guess that counts me out. I mean . . . never mind."

"He's not any threat, he's dead." Lucas met Keach's gaze.

"Oh, God, I'm sorry, Lucas." Keach's eyes filled with tears. "I don't know why I want to cry. You look so sad."

"We were married." Lucas held up his hand. "You can still see where the ring was. I took it off a year ago. My friend Sam insisted." Lucas swallowed.

"What happened to him? You don't have to tell me." Keach waited.

"He was a firefighter and he, ah . . ." Lucas swallowed. "It was a forest fire. He died trying to put it out, saved a bunch of people." Lucas sighed.

"Is that why you don't kiss on the mouth?" Keach touched his cheek.

Lucas nodded silently.

"He wouldn't mind. He'd want you to be happy. Did I make you happy?" Keach asked.

Lucas nodded. "Yes. You did. You do. Thanks."

Keach flopped onto his back. "It's the best sex I've ever had. And I thought Joe was great." He laughed. "He was the pits."

Lucas laughed with him. That was flattering.

Keach looked at him. "Can I really send Joe your picture?"

Lucas nodded. "Sure. Sock it to him."

Keach chuckled and jumped off the bed. "I'll get my phone."

Lucas stretched out, arms over his head. He turned his face into the pillow. "Go for it."

Keach took a picture, then stood staring at it. "You know, I'm not sending it."

Lucas sat up, put his legs over the side of the bed. "Okay, why not?"

"He doesn't deserve you. This picture is all mine. Do you care if I keep it?"

Lucas shrugged. "No."

It seemed like a minute later but must have been hours, because when Lucas awakened, light was peeping through the threadbare curtains.

Keach was up and dressed, working on his cell phone at the dinky table near the window. He glanced up and smiled. "Hello, sleepyhead."

For some reason, Keach's breeziness annoyed Lucas. He yawned, stretched, then tried to forget the fun they'd had the night before. "Yeah. Look, let's clean up, get some food, and get back on the road, okay?"

Keach nodded. "Sure."

Lucas picked up his phone as he headed to the bathroom.

His cell flashed two notifications — a text from Monty and one from Sam.

Monty's seemed more urgent . . .

They want to know where you are. What do I say?

. . . so he responded to that one first.

Tell them I'm following up on something.

Okay. Are you all right, Lucas?

Yeah, fine. No worries. I'll be in touch, buddy.

Sam's text was something about going out that night. Lucas knew he wouldn't be back in time to go anywhere that night. His response was short and to the point, knowing Sam would understand.

Sorry Sam, working. Talk later.

Outside, the morning was cool and fresh. A great change from the room. "I'll drive," Lucas said.

"Why? You think I'll drive us off a cliff or something?"

"I need to be at the wheel."

Keach said nothing and stayed quiet in the car as Lucas tapped in the address for Michael McKennie's lakeside cabin on his phone.

"I'm trying Mike again," Keach announced, but he soon shook his head. "Voice mail's full. He always clears his messages. I'm getting worried now."

Lucas drove a few short blocks to where Michael's house stood on Omaha Street. There was no real sign of the lake, and the street looked like the kind of neighborhood Lucas would have avoided back in LA. It looked run down, with multiple vehicles stashed on dilapidated, yellowed lawns.

The house was a shock. It was a beat-up looking brown-colored single-level box, with a weathered blue door, and a fence made of a creepy combination of chicken coop wire and spiked wooden slabs.

A dispirited looking ginger tabby cat perched, Sphinx-like, on the doorstep.

"Why are we stopping here?" Keach asked, peering out the

window across Lucas's shoulder.

"This is his house, right? I don't see much activity. No car in the driveway. I see garbage piled up out front and —"

"I have no idea where you got the idea this is Mike's house, but this isn't it," Keach said.

Lucas swiveled his head in Keach's direction. "It isn't?"

Keach shook his head. "Never seen this place before in my life."

Lucas sighed. "I'm gonna check it out. Stay here."

"But this isn't his house!"

Lucas opened the door but spotted a tall, gangly man walking along the road toward them. He was a block away, puffing on a cigarette with one hand, toting a plastic bag with groceries in the other.

Holy crap. I know this guy. If he's who I think he is, Mike McKennie's in a world of hurt.

CHAPTER FIVE

K each watched Lucas snap a photo of the guy down the street, who appeared not to notice. Lucas closed the door again, turned on the engine, and drove back the way they came.

"What's going on?" Keach twisted around in his seat to look over his shoulder.

"Is he going into the house?" Lucas asked as he pressed numbers into his cell phone.

"No. He's stopped walking. He's lighting a cigarette off the one he's been smoking. Hold on."

"He's got his cell phone out. What's the bet he's taking a photo of your car?" Lucas asked, speeding up a little. Soon the man was far behind them.

"Who is he?"

Lucas kept checking the car mirrors. "Ever hear of a guy called English, Thomas English?"

Keach glanced at him. "I don't think so."

"He had several aliases. Anglo, Britty, and—"

"Britty? Yeah, I knew Britty. Was that him? He used to be huge. Wonder how he got so thin."

"I almost didn't recognize him myself, except that he's got a distinct gait since one leg is shorter than the other."

Keach was surprised by what Lucas was saying. He had mixed feelings about Britty. "He worked with my Dad in the garage, a big guy with a ruddy face. Think he's an Irishman. Who are you calling?"

Lucas pulled over and put the call on loudspeaker. "My

Dad." Lucas waited. A few seconds later, somebody picked up the call. "Dad?"

"Lucas? Stranger. What's going on?"

"I need your help with something."

"Shoot, what's up?" his father asked.

Keach liked the man's Irish brogue. He liked Lucas, too, and wished they could have spent a few extra minutes in bed that morning. Lucas had been abrupt in his fast exit from the room, and abrasive in the way he tossed the key to the man at the front desk. Keach tried not to eavesdrop on Lucas's conversation with his dad, but it was hard.

"When you were working on that case involving the Irish mob, do you remember a guy called Thomas English?" Lucas asked his dad.

"Britty," he said, "yep, bad piece of garbage, a disgrace to the Irish. Why? He still around? Thought he was in the pen?"

"Can you find out?"

"Sure. He used to be a bodyguard to the Godfather himself. How much time I got?"

"Ah, an hour or so?" Lucas smiled. "I took a photo of him. I'll send it over to you."

"On one condition, you come for dinner. Your mother needs to see her son. She's driving me crazy."

"Agreed. Thanks." He hung up.

"Your father a cop too?" Keach asked.

"He was. Retired."

"And is your mom a good cook?"

Lucas seemed stunned. "Why do you ask?"

"I'm an orphan. Nobody to cook for me. I'm no chef, neither is my brother."

"You weren't included in the dinner invite."

Keach grinned. "Didn't say I was." *Geez, this guy is touchy.* After a beat, he asked, "So, what does Britty have to do with anything?"

"I think he was driving the getaway car in the robbery and was probably the mastermind behind it all." Lucas paused. "I'm wondering if your brother called him in a blind panic yesterday after you tried cashing that check. Look, I'm not going to lie to you, Keach. Your brother could be in a heap of shit, far more than just a robbery."

"He's in danger?" Keach asked. "That's why he's not answering the phone. Could this guy have killed Bella Boston?"

Lucas nodded. "Very likely. He has serious mob connections. The question is why? Why would he do it?" Lucas swiveled his gaze on Keach again. "The house we just visited is listed in your brother's name. That's why we went there. What a crummy dump."

"No, it wasn't. It's a typical lakeside cabin."

Lucas shot him a doubtful glance. "If you say so."

"It's true. Didn't you notice all the beautiful pine trees everywhere? It's your basic cabin, by the look of things. The rustic, unfussy style is very Tahoe."

Again, Lucas seemed unconvinced.

"This isn't Beverly Hills," Keach snapped. "People come up here to get away from all that phony stuff."

"With all those broken-down cars?"

Keach smiled. "My Dad's place looked like that. He would have loved that street. He brought all his projects up here." He narrowed his gaze at Lucas. "People come up here to be left alone. Big Bear and Arrowhead are very much like that. People can drift off the grid here." He took a deep breath. "How much do you know about my dad's business?"

"Not much." Lucas shrugged. "He was a mechanic, right?"

Keach sighed. "I need coffee."

"Me too."

Lucas made a turn off Emerald Bay Road, and Keach's toes curled with excitement in his shoes. "Oh, boy! Ernie's Coffee House is on this street, and they make awesome chocolate chip pancakes."

"I see it up ahead."

Lucas made a left turn into the parking lot of a log sided cabin that would have been the envy of anyone coveting a mountaintop home. Ernie's name was painted on a massive wooden board hanging from hinges that swayed in the early morning breeze.

Keach was out of the car in seconds. He inhaled the scent of mountain pines, loving the taste of fresh air on his tongue.

As Lucas got out and joined him, he asked, "Where is the house your brother owns?"

"Not far, but we need to talk first."

"Okay. If chocolate pancakes will get you to talk, I'm in."

Inside the coffee shop, the mingled aromas of coffee, bacon, eggs, and waffles made Keach's stomach growl.

Lucas scowled. "I never got my dollar back from Bob."

"Who's Bob?"

Lucas smiled. "Owner of the motel. He has a unique philosophy on life." He grinned even wider.

"That's a big smile," Keach observed, studying the menu in his hand.

"Yeah. Because life is short, and I still have my teeth." He held up a finger. "I actually think it even sparks a bit of joy."

Keach stared at him a moment. "Maybe it was worth losing a buck, then." He went back to the menu.

They each ordered breakfast combo specials, though Lucas opted for waffles, and Keach paid extra for chocolate chips on his pancakes. They also ordered coffees, then slid into a table in the corner.

"What is it you want to explain about your dad?" Lucas asked, sipping at the glass of iced water a waitress slid across the table to them.

"He wasn't just a mechanic."

"Oh? Why am I not surprised?"

Keach shook his head. "He was a well-respected appraiser of classic vehicles. He was hired by a lot of studio people to restore classic cars they used in movies. Sometimes he was required to locate a second, matching vehicle. One vehicle was used for close-up scenes with the actors. There was often a need for a third vehicle in case something happened to a car. He was able to build a vehicle that was identical to the original but non-operational. He ended up with garages filled with vehicle parts, and he constantly tinkered with his toys." Keach smiled at the memory. "My mom always wanted a 1967 Chevrolet Corvette L88. She was obsessed with it."

"Did he get her one?"

"He did."

Lucas seemed deep in thought. "Those are rare cars."

"Yes." *Why, oh why did I mention the damned car?*

Lucas pulled his cell phone out and was tapping away on it.

"He negotiated with the owner and had it towed to one of his garages. My dad was pimping rides before Jesse James and all those other cowboys had shows on TV restoring classic cars."

The waitress brought their food and coffee, and they paused to start eating.

"Your dad dealt with stolen cars?" Lucas glanced up and skewered him with a look.

Keach stared at his plate. "Not really. He got that car legitimately. He restored it for her. It got stolen." He remembered the dreadful fallout when his dad discovered Michael had actually been the one to remove it from the garage and sold it for a ton of money.

"What?" Lucas asked. "What are you thinking?"

"My brother was the one who stole it. Dad reported it stolen, never dreaming it was Michael. The police believed it was insurance fraud and he took the rap. Dad got two years in the can. Michael was seventeen and going through something weird. My mom never even got to drive the damn thing. My dad had it up and running. The morning he was going to give it to her, the car vanished." He forked a bite of pancake. He would never forget the chain of events. The officer involved with the case knew my dad didn't stage a robbery and kept asking *Why are you taking the rap for this?*

"Didn't it ruin his reputation?" Lucas asked.

"Yeah. In some circles. He became known as the guy who could get you rare cars. By any means necessary. Why would Dad have been so stupid?" Keach glanced at Lucas. "I never understood why he protected my brother like that."

Lucas shrugged. "I don't know. Anyway, let's swing by your brother's house. Give me the address first. I want to put off getting the state police involved. I'm going to contact a private investigator I know in Reno."

"Someone you, ah . . . slept with?" Keach asked, watching the road through the window next to him.

Lucas laughed. "No. Do you think I sleep with everyone I meet?"

Keach didn't answer right away, then he shrugged. "Pretty much. How could they resist? You're gorgeous."

Lucas reached over and squeezed his arm. "I'm a slut, but not that much of one. And this one is a woman."

"Oh." Keech started laughing.

"I just want to say that I get sick of people quickly, but I'm not sick of you."

"Thanks a lot." Keach wanted to laugh again but could tell Lucas was serious.

"Yet."

This time, Keach did laugh.

Lucas grinned and kept working on his cell phone between bites. "Your brother seems to own the property we drove by this morning. And the one you say he owns on Venice Drive."

Lucas glanced at him. "And some kind of commercial building in Reno."

"That doesn't surprise me. Reno's only an hour away from here, and it's the mini version of Vegas. I had no idea he was spending that much time up here. He always liked Vegas, and like I told you yesterday, he's mentioned financial holdings there."

Lucas kept tapping away on his phone. "I don't see anything listed under his name. Must be using a company name. Finish up. We gotta get going."

They took a couple of coffees to go and headed toward Mike's house on Venice Drive. In the distance, Harrah's Casino loomed over the lake cottages. It seemed sad to Keach. Tahoe, the biggest alpine lake in North America, was famous for its natural beauty and outdoor sports all year round in California and on the Nevada side. There had always been an argument over exactly where the dividing line was located. Officially, it was right through the middle of the lake, but to Keach, Nevada might be winning the war now that the area was home to a plethora of casinos.

"I didn't know there was a casino here," Lucas observed, as though reading his mind. "Think your brother might be there?"

"No idea." Keach shrugged. "There's quite a few casinos up here. About fifteen. My dad liked Dotty's, which is on the Nevada side of the state line. I think we should check Mike's house first."

"We're going to. He likes to gamble, right?"

Keach felt like a traitor. "Yeah."

"What's his game?"

Keach's stomach muscles clenched. "Craps. My dad taught him all about it. He used to be a lucky winner. Last I heard, he owed a few casinos money. But it's just what I heard."

Lucas threw him a shrewd look. "Your dad didn't teach

you?"

"Yeah, but I've never won. Craps is the fairest game, I think, but I don't have what it takes to gamble. I keep thinking of all the things I could buy with the money I lose. At least, I used to. I stopped trying to get money for nothing a long time ago."

"Smart guy. This is beautiful. The houses are much more high-end this side of the lake," Lucas observed.

Keach nodded. "Some of the homes are worth millions just because of the lake."

"They're still beautiful," Lucas said as his cell phone rang. He pulled over, punched the loudspeaker function on his phone. "Dad."

"Hey, son. So, I did a little digging, and like I thought, Britty's in the big house."

"So who did I see this morning?"

"Could be a family member. There are five brothers. They're all shady. I'm having one of my contacts scan the photo you sent me in the facial recognition program. By the way, Britty's serving time up in Pelican Bay. Yeah. And he had an interesting visitor yesterday. First one he's had in two years." His father paused. "It was Michael McKennie."

"Pelican Bay! Wow, that's a good seven, eight-hour drive from here." Lucas anxiously tapped the steering wheel. "He could have driven there and made it back, but he wouldn't have had time to be here already." He threw Keach an accusatory look. "Thanks, Dad. I'll get back to ya."

"Anytime. Don't forget your mom. She says she'll even make chateaubriand for you."

Keach groaned. *Chateaubriand!* His mom never made stuff like that. He recalled a childhood of frozen fish fingers and boxed macaroni and cheese. Everything she cooked came out of a box. *No wonder I like junk food.*

"That sounds good," Lucas said, taking off at a slow crawl

toward Venice Drive.

"She never offers to make it for me." Lucas's old man chuckled. "So come home soon, yeah?"

"Okay, Dad, I will." He ended the call and stopped the car across the street from Mike's house.

Keach's gaze locked on the shiny black racy Camaro sitting in the driveway. He could believe what he was seeing.

Lucas turned toward him. "From the looks of things some-one's home. You know this vehicle, right?"

"No. I know the license plate. I have no idea what this car would be doing here." Keach was alarmed, more than any-thing.

"It's a Camaro ZL1. That's a sixty-five-thousand-dollar car. TalonZ. Who or what is TalonZ?"

"My brother's ex-girlfriend." Keach felt tendrils of ice shooting through his spine. *What the hell is she doing here? Now?* It took him a second to realize he'd spoken the words aloud.

"Why?" Lucas asked. "What's the deal with her?"

"Talon Zabransky. You remember her?"

"No, sorry. Who she?" Lucas asked.

"Used to be a model. My brother was crazy about her, but they had a volatile relationship. She and I became close, and she used to call me crying about him physically abusing her."

"When was this?"

"Three years ago. It seemed so out of character for him to be abusive—"

"He may have killed his own mother, remember?"

"I doubt it. I really do. Anyway, one day, she wound up hospitalized, her face disfigured. She blamed him and came up with this horrible story about how he threw acid in her face, but the police could never find any evidence to back up her claims. She was a crack addict, and they say she got into it with some low-level drug dealer. My best friend, Robert, came with me and we checked her out of the hospital because she was afraid of Mike coming after her.

"We took her home, packed her things, and helped her leave town. We got her to a friend of Robert's, who runs a shelter for battered women." Keach swallowed. "The woman took Talon. I had to give her a thousand dollars for transportation fees and continued medical treatment. Talon had a lot of issues. But she got the help she needed. In exchange, the woman said we'd never know where she went. She said I wasn't to look for her."

"Hot damn. Yet, here she is." Lucas glanced at him. "Or is she?" A beat then he said, "Are you sure this woman helped her? Maybe she sent her off to be a sex slave someplace."

"I'm sure she helped her."

"How?"

"The woman was a nun, and the place where we took Talon was a convent in Etna."

The words hung between them.

"I'm going to check out the house," Keach said.

"I don't want you going in there alone."

"Don't worry about me. I'm a big boy. But in case I don't make it back, have a slice of Chateaubriand for me."

Lucas looked stricken. "Don't make jokes." He leaned across the space between them and kissed him.

Man, he's a good kisser. It suddenly dawned on Keach that Lucas said he never kissed anyone. The move seemed to have surprised them both.

"Fuck," Lucas said, leaning away again and letting his head fall against the headrest.

"Maybe later. No. Definitely, later." Keach got out of the car, liking that he'd made Lucas laugh. He stood, gazing at the house. It was in great shape. Better than the last time he'd seen it. Lucas soon appeared beside him. "You're coming with me?"

"Of course. Your brother has good taste, by the way."

"Sure does."

Tucked between giant pines, the A-frame redwood house looked like an elegant chalet, which it was. A wrap-around widow's walk topped a second floor, which hadn't been there the last time Keach had seen it.

"There's a lot of upgrades," Keach said. "The second floor is new, and so is the red barn in back."

They moved forward.

"There's a little kid in the driver's seat." Lucas squinted. "Holy cow, he's waving to us."

As they got closer to the house, the kid got out and ran toward them. He looked to be about two and wore nothing but a diaper. He reached Keach, hugged his knees, then did the same to Lucas, who scooped him up into his arms.

"Hello!" the kid bellowed, then put his head on Lucas's shoulder.

"Friendly tyke." Lucas grinned at Keach. "Lead the way, Kemosabe."

Keach stared at him. "Why'd you say that?" He was rattled now. Could he trust Lucas? Really?

"Just a turn of phrase. Didn't you ever watch *The Lone Ranger*?"

"Yes, but—" He bit off his own response. He'd already said too much. He could hear his father hollering at him in his mind to *keep schtum*—silent. Throughout his childhood, law enforcement of all kinds showed up at his family home and did raids at odd hours. Keach and Mike had learned to dress quickly in the dark and leash the family dogs, for fear the cops would shoot them.

"Keep schtum," their father would mutter. Not that either of his sons knew much to tell the police anyway. At least, that was what Keach always thought.

Kemosabe. He didn't want to explain that one.

They reached the front door, where a fake Christmas wreath looked the worse for wear thanks to a family of insects living in it.

Keach knocked, but the door flew open. A woman in a fancy pink kimono almost jumped from the chair standing against a low wall opposite the door. She was on her cell phone, and Keach didn't know whether to hug her or bawl at her.

"Talon. Fuck. What are you doing here?"

She was as beautiful as ever, but the acid attack had left pits in her face. Keach thought they gave her character, and they looked smoother since their last meeting, but they couldn't disguise her natural beauty. What didn't work was that she'd dyed her honey locks black.

"For fuck's sake." She got to her feet, her kimono slipping enough to reveal a white camisole beneath it. "Keach. Darling. And who's this?" She hugged Keach, then turned her lovely grey eyes to Lucas.

"Lucas. I'm a friend of Keach's. Mind telling me what your child was doing outside, unattended, behind the wheel of your car?"

She laughed. "Getting ready for the Daytona 500?" She rolled her eyes and grabbed the toddler from Lucas. "Didn't you play in the car when you were a kid? Were you ever a kid?" She adjusted the child on her hip and frowned. "I smell bacon. I can tell a pig from a mile off."

Keach was shocked by her statement.

Before Lucas could respond, the toddler leaned forward and kissed his mom's face.

"Keach. Not now." She leaned away from him and tried to put him on the ground.

The boy began to cry. "No, mama. No."

She held onto him, locking gazes with Keach. "Yeah. I named him after you." Resentment poured from her rigid stance.

"He's my nephew?"

"Yeah. Michael didn't want you to know. Say, where is he? He was supposed to meet us here last night."

"You're back together?"

"He found me. Wooed me. Married me. Knocked me up. My sister, too. Long story." She took the baby out of the room.

Lucas glanced at Keach, seeming lost for words, too.

They followed her to the kitchen, where she put the baby into a nifty-looking baby seat suspended from an antique butcher's block in the center of the room. The baby wept until she opened the fridge and removed a plastic container filled with strawberries and chopped pineapple. He stopped snuffling as he picked up pieces of fruit and squashed them into his mouth. Two rivers of snot and tears ran onto his lips.

She sighed, but some tender instinct took over, and she pulled a wad of tissues from a box on the windowsill. "Blow, baby."

He blew, and a piece of strawberry flew across the room. He laughed, and so did she, easing some of the tension between them all.

"Blow," she said again and cleared the mess on his face.

"Love you, Mama." He reached up for a kiss. She hesitated before kissing his ruby-red lips.

"I haven't seen him for six months." Talon turned hard eyes on Keach.

"Who, the baby, or his father?"

"His father. Mike took him from me eighteen months ago. My sister's been raising him with her own baby, Joshua."

"Why'd you let him do that?" Keach was in shock to discover there were so many babies in his family that he never knew about.

"I had no choice. I went to jail for tax evasion right after I gave birth. I did eight months, and when I came out, Mike had hooked up with my sister and she was pregnant. I was in no position to fight him because I had to spend a month in a half-way house. When I came out, Electra had just given birth to Joshua, and she was happy to keep the boys together."

"Unbelievable. I had no idea any of this was going on." Keach felt the surprises just kept coming.

"So your brother told me." She filled a sippy cup with bottled water and handed it to baby Keach. "I think he enjoys keeping you in the dark."

No kidding. Keach had a million questions, but he and Lucas seemed to be in sync.

"How'd you end up here?" Lucas asked. "He asked you to meet him here?"

She gave Lucas some side-eye, then said, "Yeah. He's been hiding for six months. He sent me money to go to beauty school, so apart from missing visits with my son, I was grateful for his help. He even bought me that cool car out there. Yesterday, he called me out of the blue and said Electra had gone missing with Joshua and he needed me to help him with Keach. He told me to meet him up here."

"And you saw him?" Keach asked.

"No. He was waiting for me on the highway and called me, telling me to meet him at a gas station in Placerville. I got there and was so happy to see this little guy I didn't have time to ask too many questions. Mike seemed frantic. He handed the baby over then told me he had business in Reno but to come here and lay low. He told me not to go anywhere or call anyone, but I had to go out last night and get groceries. He never called. Never showed up."

"Have you called him?" Lucas asked.

"Yes, but his voice mail is full."

Keach had found the same thing when he'd tried reaching Michael. His cell phone rang. He checked the screen. Robert.

"I gotta take this," he said and moved outside, worried

because his battery was low.

"Are you pissed about the Instagram photos?" Robert asked by way of a greeting.

"What Instagram photos?"

"Come on, guy. I know you've been glued to your social media feed."

"I haven't, as a matter of fact. My life blew apart when I tried to cash that check yesterday. I'm with the cops right now."

"Cops? What the . . . Are you for real?"

"Yes. I'm for real," Keach snapped.

"Where are you?"

"Lake Tahoe. You won't believe the shit that's been going on."

"What the eff are you doing up there?"

"Looking for my brother."

Robert paused a beat. "Oh, yeah. I remember now. He's got a place up there."

"He was supposed to come to the police station with me but never showed up. Now we're looking for him. You won't believe the—"

There was a muffled sound of voices on the other end. Keach couldn't make out the words. It was weird.

"Robert?"

"Hold on," his friend said. The line went dead.

Talon came outside. "Who are you talking to?"

"My friend Robert."

"You idiot! Tell me you're joking."

"No, I'm not joking."

"Did you tell him where you are?"

A feeling of dread cloaked Keach as he stared at her sheer terror. "Yeah," he admitted.

"I just got through telling you that Mike told me not to speak to anyone." Her eyes glittered with fury. "I should have shot you the moment you walked through the door."

"You've got a gun?" Keach asked.

"Of course." From the inside of her camisole right under her left breast, she pulled out a small gun.

"Glock subcompact .380," Lucas muttered. "Gimme that." He wrestled it from her grip.

Little Keach clung to his mother's leg and peered up fearfully as they tousled.

Lucas took the gun and checked for bullets, emptying it. "Small caliber," he said, shoving the ammo in his pants pocket, and the gun in his waistband.

"Yeah?" she jeered. "It'd still park a bullet in your brain."

"Too bad you missed your chance." His tone was light, but his cheek muscles clenched.

Keach couldn't remember Talon being so nasty. This was a woman who'd once purchased every animal in a pet store because she feared for their health in the business's deplorable conditions.

"Mama," little Keach blurted.

She ignored him.

"Mama," he implored.

"Stop it!" she ground out, glaring at big Keach.

"Mama!"

"I can't believe you told that idiot Robert where you are." Talon was whipping herself into a frenzy.

"He's my friend. You know him."

"Yeah? And you trust him? You really had no idea he and Mike have been on the down-low for over a decade?"

"I—"

"He even balled your boyfriend."

"Who? My brother or Robert?"

She gave a harsh laugh. "Robert. Maybe Mike, too. But I caught Robert and Joe in my bed. Mike was busy in the kitchen, making eggs. Very cozy. I went nuts. That was the first time I punched your brother in the face." Her face took on a nasty gleam. "How is Joe, by the way?"

"Enough," Lucas said, his voice low, but his tone menacing enough to make her stop talking. "You really think this Robert guy is involved in something . . . deadly?"

"I know he is. And we all need to get out of here." She glared at Keach. "You just signed my death warrant. You stupid, stupid man."

CHAPTER SIX

K each was stunned by Talon's words. She was incoherent after that. She cried, which made the baby cry.

Lucas tried to calm her. "Tell us what's going on."

"I can't. I can't tell you. I have to get out of here."

"Mama," the baby whined and began to pee right where he stood, overflowing his diaper.

"Ugh." Talon dragged him by the hand down the hall. The baby left a trail of pee in his wake.

"She has to come with us," Lucas said to Keach.

"Where are we going?" Keach's mind was in a twirly whirl. When would the ride stop? He tried to wrap his head around the idea of the three most important men in his life having a gang bang.

Without me. They've been laughing at me for years. Not Robert. I can't believe it. Not. Robert. He would never hurt me like that. He was trying to think if there's been times he couldn't find Joe or Robert. Not many. He winced at the thought that they had been carrying on and he'd had no idea. He tried to think of the times they'd all been together. Had there been long looks? Shared whispers? Any sign of flirtation?

None.

"You okay?" Lucas asked.

"Not really."

From inside the bathroom, Talon screamed, "Stop it!"

"Motherhood doesn't suit everybody," Lucas drolled.

Keach followed Lucas down the hallway, his mind still reeling.

Lucas knocked on the door. "Everything okay in there?" No response. The yelling had stopped, and the ensuing silence was ominous. Lucas knocked again. "Talon?" He tried the bathroom door handle. Locked. "Talon?" he called again. There was commotion on the other side of the door, then it stopped. Lucas put his ear to the door. "Shit. She just opened the window. She's trying to escape." He ran toward the back door, Keach hot on his tail. Locked. No way to open it. Lucas ran around the house and came back with the key, which was dangling from a keychain with a toy gun hanging from it.

Door unlocked, they raced outside. The backyard was huge, with a covered pool, a boat, tiki bar, multiple fire pits, massive barbecue, and several motorbikes covered in heavy, protective wraps.

"This looks like my dad's place used to," Keach said. They looked to the left, then the right and split up. Where the hell had she gone?

"I don't hear anything," Lucas whispered, meeting up with Keach near the red barn. "I thought she'd head straight for her car."

It took some maneuvering, but they made their way toward it, squeezing past hoses and stacks of tools to reach the driveway. Talon was at the left rear door of her Camaro, the baby on her hip.

She locked gazes with Keach. "Wait!" he shouted.

He and Lucas still had to wedge past more obstacles to get to her. They stumbled over boxes and crates.

Talon looked panic-stricken. She still wore her kimono, and the baby wore nothing. He'd been in a diaper up until now. He let out a loud wail.

"Talon. Don't be a fool. Come with us," Lucas yelled.

"And get killed?" she called over her shoulder. She plonked the baby in a child seat on the backseat, then got behind the wheel just as Lucas reached her.

"You've got a distinctive car," Lucas said, trying to stop her from closing her door. "Leave it here and come with us."

"Fuck you!" She kicked out at him, started the engine, and took off with the driver's side door swinging open in her wake.

"I'll ride with you," Keach said, as Lucas stood there, hands on hips.

"You need to call your friend Robert," Lucas said. "See if he knows anything about Mike. Why was he calling you, anyway?"

"We talk every day." Keach felt defensive. "We got cut off—" His phone rang again. "It's him." He took the call, but Robert didn't say a word. Ominous scratching noises in the background terrified him.

"Hang up," Lucas said. "We need help."

No shit!

They crossed the road back to Keach's car. Somebody had keyed it all the way along the driver's side.

Lucas stared at it. "Good times," he deadpanned and got behind the wheel. As he started the engine, Keach opened the glove compartment and removed his phone charger. He attached it to his cell phone and plugged it into the outlet on his console.

"Good idea," Lucas said. "We'll take turns. I see we both have iPhones."

"Right." Keach was distressed. The whole scene with Talon had unnerved him. "I'm worried about the baby," he blurted.

"I understand." Lucas's phone rang, and he blew out a sigh. "That's my boss. They've been calling me for the last twenty minutes and I keep ignoring them." He took the call, turned off the engine, and stepped outside, holding up his right index finger to Keach.

Lucas paced outside, and Keach opened the passenger door. Snatches of the conversation drifted his way.

"But I am on the trail. I've found out a lot. He's got

property in Tahoe . . ." Then, "He seems to be missing. Keach McKennie can't reach him. Yeah, he's been calling him since last night." Then, "Reno? Well, we're close. I know somebody there." A beat. "You sure it was him? Okay. I'm on it."

Lucas returned to the car, and Keach closed his door again. Lucas got inside, frowning.

"Your brother was in Reno last night. Got eighty-sixed from a club there. Drunk and disorderly. Two bouncers drove him away from there. Reno PD can't locate him, or the bouncers."

"That's bad news." Keach swallowed. "Which club?"

"Some nightclub that's part of a multi-use building. They're still searching for him."

"That's weird. It sounds like Hummingbird, which is his own club. I know he bought a commercial space, opened the two top floors for luxury residential space. The rest of the building is offices, a day spa, the club, and a couple of high-end boutiques."

"What's the building called?" Lucas glanced at him.

"Harper Inc."

"Harper, after your mother?"

"Yeah."

"But I thought your brother hated her?"

"A lot went on between them after my father died that they never openly revealed to me. She invested in his business but never said much to me. I just listened and kept schtum. That was my father's favorite word."

"So they excluded you."

Keach nodded. It hurt like hell that his mom had banded with Mike after Keach's falling out with Michael Sr. And yet, when she was in trouble or needed help, she'd reach out to him.

"Your father sounds like a character straight out of a British TV crime series."

Keach grinned. "My father was Irish. He spent half his life pretending he wasn't because he didn't think being Irish was classy. And he spent the other half letting some people think he was some kind of Irish mobster."

"Well, he was, wasn't he?"

Keach was silent. When he thought of the wise guys who'd populated his childhood, he realized his dad qualified as a mobster.

"You didn't give me this much detail before." Lucas's tone was accusatory.

"I . . . I was being protective toward my brother. My dad never wanted to tell anyone, especially law enforcement, anything about family business."

"He had a lot to hide." Lucas started the engine and unplugged Keach's phone, attaching his own phone to the charging cable.

"Most adults do," Keach said. His phone rang again. Robert. He took the call, but the line went dead.

"Probably." Lucas kept the engine running but made no effort to drive. "I think I know someone who can help us." He kept his phone charging and said, "I'm calling Amanda Delany. She once worked for the LAPD. She was a great cop but got fed up with the bullshit. She moved to Reno and started her own PI agency. Now she's got offices in Reno and Laughlin." He put his phone on loudspeaker as the phone rang. "I hear she spends most of her time in Reno."

"All the Nevada gambling hot spots. She must be making a fortune," Keach said.

The woman picked up on the third ring. "You son of a bitch. Where are you, Luke?"

"On the road, headed your way, Juicy Fruit." Lucas smiled.

She laughed. "No one dares call me that but you, you big queer."

"And you are the only one who can call me that and live

another day." He laughed.

She chuckled. "I miss you, my pal. What's up? You finally come to your senses and decide to join me out here in Fantasy Land?"

"Afraid not. I may need your help on something. I'm looking for a guy by the name of Mike McKennie. Heard of him? Got a place out at Lake Tahoe."

"Yep. Likes to play with some of the wise guys here in Reno. Owes a shitload of money, from what I heard."

Lucas glanced at Keach, who couldn't disguise his surprise.

"What's going on?" she asked.

"He was supposedly thrown out of a club last night in your neck of the woods."

"You talking about the Hummingbird kidnapping?"

It was Lucas's turn to gape. "You know about that?"

"Yeah."

"I'm with his brother, Keach McKennie. It's a long story, but we'd like to come up there."

"Where are you?"

"Tahoe."

"Ah. So you're an hour away." She seemed to be rustling papers.

"How did you know he was kidnapped?"

"Got a call from Nevada PD. Apparently he was double-dipping. Playing with the gangsters and also being a snitch. You know how popular those guys are."

Keach ran a hand over his face. *So it was Hummingbird. Oh, boy. Didn't he know the meaning of keeping schtum?*

Amanda continued. "Some big case he was right in the middle of. Drugs and luxury cars. I just farmed out the kidnapping case to one of my PIs. You know how much I hate leaving my comfortable chair."

Lucas laughed.

"Come on up to my office. I'll give you a hand," she said.

"Perfect," he replied and hung up.

"Juicy Fruit?" Keach glanced at him.

He shrugged, put the car into gear, then pulled out onto the road.

"We're heading to Reno then?" Keach was anxious.

Lucas smiled. "Yeah. I like playing chauffeur. What the hell. I'll take it out in trade later."

"You said that with a serious face." Keach reached over and touched his cheek. He stroked Lucas's face for a second and smiled. "You're a good cop. I feel safe with you."

"Good."

"My heart, not so much."

Lucas didn't comment.

"Are you going to tell me why you're not working homicide? You were a homicide cop, weren't you, you and this Juicy Fruit woman."

Lucas nodded. "Yes. She left out of protest when I got busted down to the Bunko Squad."

"What happened?"

Lucas took a breath. "My Lieutenant wanted to sleep with me."

"He was gay?"

"In the closet, married, kids. I wasn't interested at all. He didn't like that."

"Oh, baby," Keach murmured.

Lucas smiled. "To make a long story short, I went higher up, but they didn't believe me. I'd been married to a man. I was out of the closet and not shy about it. They believed him, Mr. Respectable. Even after I was transferred, a lot of people didn't want to work with me. I'd been pegged as a trouble-maker, a liar. So, here I am."

"That prick still there?" Keach demanded. He couldn't help his angry tone.

Lucas nodded. "One day he'll get caught. I was an easy

target. After I lost Christopher, I became careless, a risk-taker, and when I was booted out of homicide, I really thought it was the end of everything."

"You still feel that way?" Keach kept his tone soft.

Lucas hesitated a moment, then he said, "Things are looking up."

He leaned forward and planted a soft, quick kiss on Keach's mouth.

Keach was delighted. "That was nice. Wow."

"That was just the beginning. I'm renowned for my kissing. Maybe I could even spring for a hamburger later and then give you a demonstration?"

"Honey, go for a steak," Keach licked his lips. "I could kiss you all night long."

Lucas winked at him, then suddenly stopped the car.

"What?" Keach demanded, then looked at where Lucas was staring. "Damn. It's Talon's car."

They pulled up behind the vehicle, but nobody seemed to be inside it.

"Stay here," Lucas insisted.

Keach scoffed. "As if."

They approached the vehicle. It was eerie. The keys were in the ignition, and the radio was playing the Bob Marley song, *No Woman No Cry*. Both Talon and the baby were gone.

"Weird," Lucas said.

Suddenly a whoosh of wind and sound came so close they dived for cover between the two vehicles. Keach looked up and saw a classic Thunderbird blow past them.

"That's the guy we saw walking toward the first house this morning!" Lucas shouted, taking a photo with his cell phone. From the passenger seat, Talon reached out laughing, giving them the finger.

"The baby's in the backseat, right?" Keach asked.

"Looks like it."

Lucas called South Lake Tahoe police, and Keach marveled at the way he reported Talon's abandoned vehicle and the man who had her in the Thunderbird.

"She gave me the finger," Lucas told the emergency dispatcher. "Real polite. I don't think she's under duress, but since a small child's involved, I thought it best to report it." He smiled with smug satisfaction as he ended the call.

Keach and Lucas waited for fifteen minutes for the local cops to arrive.

They were pleasant enough, but since neither Lucas nor Keach had witnessed the alleged abduction, they were asked to vacate the scene.

"With pleasure," Lucas responded, rolling his eyes so only Keach could see. Back in the Prius, Lucas said, "Let's drive by the house from this morning and see what's up." Seconds later his cell phone rang, and he glanced at it quickly. "Got a photo." He showed Keach. "This is the man who visited Britty in jail yesterday. Is this your brother?"

Keach's heart sank. "Yeah. Do they have any idea why he went?"

Lucas tapped something into his phone. "Not yet."

They drove back to the original house, but there was no sign of activity. Even the cat from earlier in the morning was gone.

"Somebody's been here," Lucas said. "There's bags of rubbish by the bins." He opened up a sack. "No bodies. No weapons. Bad eating habits. They like Twinkies. Just like you." He closed the bag again.

Keach didn't argue the point. He didn't like Twinkies much. He'd eat them in an emergency, but he preferred chocolate junk cakes.

They walked around a bit, but when they looked in the windows, the house was empty. There wasn't a stick of furniture in any of the rooms.

"Somebody was camping here," Lucas said. "This has all the signs of a drop house. Wonder who the guy was that we saw?"

"Well, the police are after him now," Keach said. "Maybe we'll find out."

Back in the Prius, they headed north to Reno. Lucas switched phones on the charger and made a call to somebody that seemed to be in code.

It gave Keach's mind time to think about everything that had happened in the last twenty-four hours.

Harper McKennie had always told people she stayed with her husband for Keach. But even when he was grown and out of the house, she didn't leave Michael Sr. When he had a very public affair with his personal assistant, his mom believed she needed to wait it out.

"I'll always take care of you, Harper," Dad had said to her over dinner one night with Michael Jr., Keach, *and* the mistress at a Hollywood steak house. It was a cheap and tacky meal, just like his grubby affair.

Harper had stayed for the money. *Dad lulled her into a false sense of security.*

"He needs me," she'd said at the time. "He acts all macho, but he couldn't look after himself if his life depended on it." It had devastated her when he moved out and asked for time to *find himself.* When he decided the mistress was getting too demanding, he threw a little love Harper's way, and things were okay until he eyed a younger, boobier prize.

After his death, Harper had struggled to survive as she coped with the shocking news that her husband had drained all their bank accounts.

Where had the money gone?

Somehow, she'd had a windfall she'd never explained. Then came her secretive investments with Mike.

Keach was the one who paid her day-to-day bills up until

then. He'd hired a forensic accountant to do a paper chase, much to the fury of Michael, who said it was a waste of money. Was it? Or was Michael afraid of something else?

Keach had still paid for the accountant, who couldn't find the missing funds.

What else had his dad been up to?

Suddenly, things were making sense, small moments he'd questioned over the years,

And it was disturbing.

His mother had died a little over a year ago, and it had been devastating. She's told him her investment with Mike had failed but never explained — it was the old schtum routine once more. She'd had a headache that turned out to be brain cancer. Within three weeks she was gone.

"You're awfully quiet," Lucas said and pulled off the highway.

"Where are we going?"

"Just a little detour." Lucas parked the car between a stand of tall pines. A dark, quiet space to do dirty things. Lucas switched off the engine. "For future reference. Get a bigger car next time. Priuses might be good for the ecology, but this one could do my back in." As he climbed over and moved on top of Keach, they both let out a breath.

"I'll keep that in mind," Keach murmured against Lucas's mouth.

Lucas dragged him into the back seat, making Keach laugh.

"This reminds me of being with my first boyfriend and having sex in his dad's car," Keach said.

Lucas frowned. "You had car sex with another guy? Who is he? I'll find him and kill him."

"No need." Breathing was becoming difficult.

Keach huffed in harsh gusts as Lucas sat on the small bench seat and pulled Keach onto his lap. He pushed Keach back, so he was reclining, then stared, fixated, at Keach's crotch.

Lucas licked his lips and buried his face in the fabric of Keach's jeans, rubbing his lips and cheeks against Keach's hardening cock. "Gifts," he murmured and unbuttoned the fly.

Keach's head fell back. *Yes, oh yes. God. Please.* He stifled a cry as Lucas reached into the fly and moved Keach's boxer briefs aside, pulling out his cock. He held it in his fist, slapping it against his open mouth.

"Your cock is perfect," Lucas drawled.

That was weird. Joe always said it was average. *What the hell did I see in him?*

Lucas sucked in his length, and his mouth felt amazing. It was like it had been made for him. Keach ran his hands under Lucas's shirt sleeves. His skin was smooth and . . . oh . . . Keach squirmed when he noticed the boner beneath his ass. Lucas was hard. For a moment, Lucas released him, and Keach's pink cockhead glistened.

He couldn't stop thinking about how nice last night had been. The man was perfect. Just perfect. He knew he was going to spend hours pleasuring Lucas, and couldn't wait to begin.

Keach's cock was so hard it was sticking up toward his belly. He felt suddenly shy, but Lucas touched his cock with reverent fingers and swallowed his shaft in one strike. He wedged his fingers between Keach's jeans and his ass and drew his lips slowly back up his shaft. He stroked Keach's hole, over and over, while he pulled his mouth all the way up, keeping just his lips on the cock head, then plunged back down again. Keach's balls grazed the knuckles of Lucas's right hand, and the man stopped sucking on Keach's cock to pay them his respects.

It drove Keach crazy. Lucas's hand working on his ass, his thumb probing Keach's guiche, and two fingers in his ass. As he did this, he swabbed Keach's balls with his insistent tongue. Keach could barely breathe. He rocked his hips, trying to fight his way back inside Lucas's mouth.

"Suck me," Keach begged in a husky voice as he came so hard and fast . . . so hard, it was like being hit by a tidal wave inside his body. He groaned as Lucas released him.

Lucas grinned. "To be continued." He took long licks of Keach's still rigid shaft, cleaning up every last drop of come.

"To be continued *now*," Keach rasped.

Lucas chuckled. "Later, gator. We gotta get moving." He moved back into the driver's seat, Keach scrambling to return to the passenger side. "We steamed up the windows." Lucas grinned as Keach kissed him, then his cell phone rang. "It's Amanda Day." He took the call. "We're on our way," he said, putting the call on speakerphone.

"You'd better hurry," she said. "And keep Keach McKennie safe. I just heard from Pelican Bay. They have a recording of the conversation yesterday between Mike McKennie and Thomas English. You're not gonna like this. Britty was asking Mike to do a hit for him. And he agreed."

"Who's the target?" Lucas asked.

"Keach McKennie."

CHAPTER SEVEN

"What do we do now?" Keach asked, panicked at the idea that his own kin wanted him ... *dead*. He glanced around, hoping not to see Britty, his brother, or anybody else associated with them striding past with an Uzi pointed at him.

"What we do now is have a slight freak out," Lucas said.

"*Slight* panic?"

"Well, yeah." He pulled off to the shoulder of the highway, switched off the motor, and slumped in the driver's seat. "There's always a plan."

"And you have one?" The idea cheered up Keach immensely.

"Not as such. But the way I figure it, we're both in trouble. I don't think we're going to die. Not when I'm in such a great mood." He grinned at Keach. "That's some hot sex we're having and I, for one, plan on keeping at it. Practice makes perfect, right?"

"Ah, right. Yeah."

"And we can't be dead if we plan on it. Right?"

Is he crazy? "Right." *I have to trust this guy. I think.*

"So we need to stick together." Lucas started singing the lyrics from Roxy Music's *Let's Stick Together*. He snapped his fingers and shimmied in his seat.

I love that song! Wait. What am I thinking? Man, is this guy nuts or what? Why do I keep attracting frickin' weirdoes?

Lucas stopped singing. "I told you I was in a good mood. I'm a pretty good singer."

No, you're not.

"But I'm bad at love. I've been in a rotten mood for three years. I don't even sing in the shower anymore. Everything pisses me off." Lucas drummed his fingers on the steering wheel. "So, as I see it, we have a couple of problems here. The first one is your ex-boyfriend, Joe."

Keach squinted at him. "How is he a problem?"

"He's orbiting you."

"He's . . . what?"

"Orbiting you. You haven't heard of it?"

"No. What the hell is it?"

"The new term the kids are using for stalking your ex online. I blame myself for letting you post the photo of us on your Instagram page. It's unglued him. I've noticed you don't check your social media much. He's addicted to it. He went bonkers when you posted that photo."

"How do you know?"

"While you were sleeping this morning, I looked at your Instagram. He posted three comments."

"How weird. He doesn't care about me at all. What did he say?"

Lucas sighed. "He calls me your boy toy. I've been called worse, but there's nothing plastic about me. I'm no toy. I wasn't made in Taiwan. I'm a man. And he's a halfwit."

In spite of his fears, Keach laughed.

"There's no identifying background images that give away our location—"

"You think he knows where we are?"

Lucas stared straight ahead as cars zoomed past them. "He posted a nasty comment, *How'd you like cheap motels?*"

"Oh. Shoot. I had no idea."

Lucas shrugged. "I thought it was a lucky guess and aimed at making you feel bad." He frowned. "Is that his stock in trade?"

"Lately, yeah." *How could I not have realized how awful he was* before *we broke up?*

Lucas nodded. "He could be involved but—"

"What about Talon?"

"She may have been lying about being afraid of Michael. She could have let him know we're in Tahoe, but the conversation Michael had with Britty was yesterday." He paused. "I believe he knew *yesterday* that we were here and the only way that could have happened is if he's tracking you."

"Oh, God." Keach blinked, trying to compute it all. "He used to monitor me via that app, Find My Friends, but I disabled it a long time ago."

"You need to check." When Keach hesitated, Lucas growled, "Check it *now*."

Keach searched through his phone for the app. "Holy crap. He's put the tracking option back on my phone. Or somebody has. I don't recognize this number. Oh . . ." Keach felt faint.

Lucas reached over and squeezed his shoulder. "What?"

"It's Joe's number. He has two cell phones. This one's a pay as you go. I only know it because he called his new boyfriend from it. Weeks before we broke up. Joe and I were on the same cellular plan, and I paid the bills." He felt a stab of fury as he took his name off the tracking list. "He must have grabbed hold of my phone and put my number back on his app."

"Did you deactivate it?"

"Yeah."

"Good. He's jealous as hell that you're involved with someone else. Even if he was the one who left you in the first place."

Keach shook his head. "That's crazy."

"I'm gonna need to call my boss. This thing's gotten way outta control." Lucas snatched his phone from the console where he'd been charging it and got out of the car.

Keach plugged his own phone in and watched as his new lover paced the shoulder of the highway talking into his phone. Keach's phone beeped, and he checked the screen.

Are you sure you want to proceed?

He blinked. *Damn.* He thought he'd already removed himself from the app.

"Damn bippy I'm sure." He jabbed at the yes option and waited. Relief spread through him when he received confirmation that he was now no longer findable by his alleged friends.

When did he start tracking me again? Boy, am I a dunce. I had no idea he'd done this again. Not after the raging fight we had when I first found out he was following my movements. Why did he do this? Did he think I was having an affair?

Then the thought hit him like a brick to the head. *No. He was keeping track of me because he was the one having the affair. I bet he was keeping a watchful eye that I didn't come home and discover him in bed with his piece of euro trash. Ugh. What if they had sex in our bed?*

Lucas returned, a focused look in his eyes as he started the car once again. He pulled out onto the road with a screech of tires.

"What's the plan?" Keach asked.

"We go to Tahoe. We pick up bulletproof vests. I've been ordered to switch out to an unmarked police cruiser."

"You mean I leave my car in Tahoe?"

"Yeah. Sorry. It's too distinctive. It'll be safe. Then we head back to LA."

"And we leave my car up here?"

"For now."

"And we go back to LA for what reason? To be sitting ducks?"

"No. We go back to LA because I've been ordered to return. Since there's a hit out on you, I'm instructed to take you to a safe house." Lucas switched lanes, cutting off two women in a VW bug that had seen better days. Their mouths opened in unheard screams that Lucas didn't notice.

"We're taking the 395," he muttered as he glanced over his shoulder to check that the next lane change was okay."

"Fine," Keach said, but it wasn't. *I just had to go cash that check yesterday.* He mentally slapped himself upside the head.

Lucas suddenly swerved to the shoulder and kept his foot on the brake. They surged forward from the impact of the move. "Gimme your cell phone. Wanna make sure your ex hasn't put a tracking device on it."

Keach handed it over.

With a grim expression on his face, Lucas took the battery out and examined the phone. "Huh. Nothing. It must have been that stupid app. I didn't know it had such a huge range." He glanced at Keach, the look in his eyes frightening. "Unless he's been tracing you and followed you up here. Looks like your ex is involved, too."

"I . . ." Keach had no response to that. He didn't think Joe would get involved in anything illegal. But then again, he never would have expected Joe to have a threesome with Michael, either.

Lucas put the phone back together, and they jumped when Keach's cell phone rang.

"It's Joe," Keach said. "Why's he calling me?"

Lucas gave him a grimace. "Because he just figured out you disabled that stupid app. Don't answer it. But it gives me an idea."

He swung back out into traffic and hooked a right on the next exit. He took a series of sharp turns, muttering and cursing as they wound up back onto Omaha Street, at the very first house they'd been to that belonged to Michael. The ginger tabby cat was back on the front porch, loitering on the doormat. Garbage still spilled out over the over-stuffed bins near the driveway, but the place looked deserted.

"C'mon, let's go look around," Lucas said, as he parked the car across the road from the dilapidated property.

They walked across the street, and the ginger cat ignored them as they walked around the side of the house. Just like the ritzier property Michael owned, the backyard was filled with all kinds of vehicles. There were a couple of snowmobiles Keach knew would be put to use in the winter months. They spotted a huge metal container with several locks on it.

"Aw, geez. I hope there isn't a naked woman chained up in there," Lucas said. "I watched the whole TV report on that serial killer, Todd Kohlhepp, and his victim, Kala Brown. Kept her in a storage container for months and claimed it was consensual." He looked around. "I need bolt cutters."

"Is it legal for you to cut the locks?"

Lucas glanced at him as he picked his way through numerous buckets of tools until he found the one he wanted. "In my experience, it's always easier to ask for forgiveness afterward than to get permission before." He cut the four locks on the container. They pinged off in several different directions.

"Oops," Lucas said. He pried open the door, and they peered inside. "Huh." He wiped his brow. "Now I know how the people who opened Al Capone's vault felt."

"I'm glad, actually. I'd prefer to see nothing inside than a dead body. Or a chained up live one." Keach stepped back as Lucas slammed the door shut.

"What did you hope to find?" Keach asked.

Lucas shrugged, a distressed look on his face. "Some fancy stolen car, maybe. This is all about classic cars, money, and I'll bet drugs."

"Oh, the unholy trinity," Keach murmured.

"Something like that." Lucas gave him a wan smile. "It sure is a lot easier on *Hawaii Five-O*. Those guys luck out all the time." He turned and headed back to the car, Keach trotting to keep up with him. "Have you noticed how they always find parking right outside the place they need to be? They never get stuck at traffic lights—"

"I've never noticed, to be honest. I'm too busy checking out the hot guys."

They reached the car. Lucas unlocked the doors. "Which one do you like?"

"McGarrett, of course." Keach hopped into the passenger seat as Lucas took the wheel.

"People say I look like him." Lucas started the engine.

If you say so. Keach fought the urge to laugh. "I'm sure they do."

"Are you making fun of me?"

"Just a little."

Lucas shook his head as he drove away from the house. "No respect. That's what I get."

Keach reached over and touched his thigh. "You're much better looking than he is."

Lucas frowned. "Why'd you have to go and say that when I can't do anything about it?"

Keach laughed. "Let's save the mushy stuff for later."

"It wasn't going to be mushy. It was going to be hard and fast and—"

Keach's cell phone rang. "Shoot. I gotta take it. It's the office." He'd done no work for a few days and had been worrying about follow-up calls to prospective clients that still hadn't been made. Lucas was focusing on the road, but Keach was certain he would be listening avidly to his conversation. Unfortunately, it was a call from one of his diligent, least warm and fuzzy account managers.

"Dude," Warren Orr said across the miles. He was a toffee-nosed Brit with an accent that did *not* go with a word like *dude*. "I don't know how you did it, but Sir Bob Geldof is doing interviews talking about how he's signed up for a ticket to the moon."

"I didn't have anything to do with it. Bob Geldof signed up before I joined the company."

Warren didn't seem to be listening. "His interviews led to two other bookings. Don't you check your emails? They specifically mention you. But since they're British passengers, you're going to have to share the sale with, er, ah, me. We'll split the commission."

Typical Warren, sticking his fancy shoes in other people's business. Keach said nothing. He hadn't checked emails except for looking for communication from his brother. Warren went on and on, and Keach realized the guy had commandeered his sale and was calling to give him a heads-up, as well as informing him in a polite way that he wouldn't be able to challenge losing commissions that were rightfully his. He let Warren ramble, wondering who on earth had emailed the company crediting Keach with inspiring them to purchase tickets to outer space.

"I'm sure you're busy nailing that next big catch. I'll let you get back to it. Byeee!" Warren ended their call.

Lucas was staring wide-eyed at Keach. "Bob Geldof, *the* Bob Geldof is going to the moon?"

"Yeah." Keach frowned as he rifled through his email messages. *My God. The spam.* He had numerous offers to improve the size of his manhood, as well as pet massage tools. Since he didn't have a pet, he'd happily delete them but didn't have time right now. *I could use a damned massage myself.*

"What other famous people have tickets for this gig?"

Keach swiveled a glance at Lucas. "Lots of 'em. Lady Gaga, Katy Perry, Leonardo DiCaprio, Tom Hanks, Brad Pitt, Justin Bieber—"

"They need to maroon Justin Bieber out there."

"That's not nice. He says such great things about you."

Lucas laughed. "You're ridiculous."

"Where are we going?" Keach asked as they pulled into Venice Drive and pulled up outside Mike's swankier abode. Once again, Lucas parked across the road from the house. He switched off the engine, leaned back in his seat and eyed the massive wood and glass structure. It seemed to sparkle in the sun. "I dunno how to explain it, but even though this house looks beautiful and it's certainly in better shape than the other one, this place really creeps me out."

"I know what you mean." Keach peered across Lucas's shoulder at the house.

Together, they stepped out of the car and moved across the road.

"Let's check the barn," Lucas said.

That was the moment Keach realized Lucas still held the bolt cutters from the first house.

Keach gestured to it. "Isn't that stealing?"

"You think your brother's gonna have me arrested for it?"

"Prolly not."

They reached the barn, and once again, Lucas cut the lock on the door. Thankfully there was nothing inside except the faint trace of a terrible smell.

"Death," Lucas murmured.

"Are you sure?"

"Sure as I can be." Lucas's cell phone rang as they shut the door again. He checked the screen. "That's my boss." He took the call and strode away from Keach who didn't know what to do with himself. He walked back to his car and got behind the wheel. He was a lousy backseat driver and felt better whenever he had control over his own vehicle. He went through his cell phone again, hunting for the emails Warren had been talking about.

He opened the first one. To his utter amazement, his brother had bought another ticket to outer space, crediting Keach's fine salesmanship as the reason.

Is he kidding me? He already has a ticket. Why's he buying a second? And why didn't he go through me?

Keach's cell phone kept pinging as he worked through his junk mail to find the second booking. Annoyed, he checked the text message associated with it. Joe had left two messages.

Where you at?

You need to call me ASAP.

For Joe, this was profound communication.

Lucas turned up seconds later and got into the passenger seat. "Ready for Reno?"

"I guess. I just found out something weird."

"What's that?"

"I just got a booking through the British headquarters and—"

"Lemme guess. Your brother made the booking."

"How'd you figure that out?"

Lucas shrugged, his expression grim. "He's covering his tracks. By singing your praises and signing up for another ride, he's showing his support of you." His eyes turned bleak as he added, "He doesn't want anyone to know he's activated a hit out on you. And he's willing to spend a quarter of a million dollars to prove it. Geez, babe, you're in more trouble than I thought."

CHAPTER EIGHT

Lucas practiced his inner smile all the way to Reno. The old man at the motel had made it look so damned easy. Lucas's mind flicked back and forth between the crazy events of the last twenty-four hours, and the astonishing news his lieutenant had just given him. The facts whirled around in Lucas's head, making driving difficult.

Lieutenant Evan Pringle had made it clear that he wasn't to break the news to Keach yet. He wanted another member of law enforcement present when that happened. Pringle knew Amanda Delany and said he'd clear it with her and make sure she was there when Lucas broached the subject with him.

"Another set of eyes and ears won't hurt," Pringle had said. "Besides, he might already know."

"I doubt it," Lucas had said on the street outside Mike McKennie's house, pacing back and forth before rejoining Keach in the car. "You've admitted yourself he isn't involved. Not a single piece of evidence links back to him. He had no clue what he was about to unleash trying to cash that damned check."

"Possibly," Pringle allowed.

"And if you hadn't brought his friend Robert Rymer in for questioning, we might never have known the extent of all the deception. And, by the way, there are things we still don't know." Lucas had hesitated before saying more, and Pringle had fallen silent.

As Lucas sped upcountry toward Reno, he tried to figure

out why Britty wanted Keach dead. And would Mike go along with it? Did he know about . . . *What a mess. I can't believe how quickly this case has erupted into one giant stink hole.*

It was his fault things had evolved between him and Keach, not that he had any regrets. On the contrary, just thinking about the guy made him feel warm and fuzzy.

Inconceivable! I'm not that kinda guy. But I like this sparky feeling. I won't think of it as joy. It's just a happy feeling. A good thing. God, now I sound like Martha Stewart. It's a good thing!

He kept thinking positive thoughts, as positive as he could be, anyway. Pringle had asked a lot of questions about why he'd left town with Keach. And, while Lucas had responded, it had been clear his lieutenant thought it was Lucas's fault that their drive to Tahoe had put Keach in danger.

"Everything okay?" Keach asked.

"Yeah. Why?" Lucas snapped.

Keach shrugged. "Well, you've been anxious since we got in the car, and you keep checking the mirrors. You think we're being followed?"

Lucas was surprised that Keach had noticed what he'd thought was furtive checking. No. He didn't think they were being followed, not that he said so. He saw Keach making a call. "Who're you trying to reach?"

"Bobby. Sorry, I have to keep reminding myself he likes to be called Robert now. He's not answering, and I didn't like the way our conversation ended."

That's because the police were at his door. That was another thing. Everyone in Keach's life seemed to be embroiled in this mess. *How far is Keach involved?*

He focused on the drive until they made it to Reno in forty-seven minutes. Maybe Keach hadn't noticed how fast Lucas had been driving. He barely spoke to Keach because his mind was too busy spinning. Besides, he kept fielding calls from Pringle, who left terse texts every few minutes saying *Call me.*

Lucas sailed through the entrance to the city, marked by a

sweeping overhead blue and white arc of a sign reading *Biggest Little City In The World*. He swiveled his gaze everywhere, surprised at how quaint and peaceful it seemed. Like Vegas probably was fifty years ago. There were telltale signs of what some people considered progress. New buildings and massive malls were going up everywhere, interspersed with quaint offices and shops, including a multitude of casinos. The same sign appeared in red, white, and pink over one of them.

"It has a lot more nature than Vegas, doesn't it?"

"More trees, anyway." Keach twisted in his seat. "Why do I have a sinking feeling in my stomach?"

Lucas said nothing, keeping his gaze on the traffic. He had no idea how to break the news he had to Keach, or even how the guy would take it. He heaved a sigh and veered off Johnson Boulevard to a sprawling outdoor mall bordering the local police station. Every building in the vicinity was painted brown and sported huge glass windows. The massive pine trees lining every available inch only added to woodsy feel to it all.

Amanda Delany's office was tucked between a drugstore on one side and a department store outlet on the other. She even had wooden shutters that closed her off from the world. Lucas parked in one of the spaces in front.

He turned off the engine and glanced at Keach. "It's gonna be okay," he said, not knowing why he said it, or even if it was true.

Keach didn't respond as they got out of the car.

Amanda's door opened, and Lucas half expected her to mosey on out with a wheat stalk dangling from her lips.

"Well, of all the gin joints in all the world," she joked. "How are you, lucky pants?"

Lucas laughed, stepped forward to hug her, then turned to glance at Keach. Out of the corner of his eye, he spotted a police car rolling in behind them. One officer got out, the driver blocking Keach's Prius from being able to reverse out of the parking space if he chose to do so.

Keach gazed back at Lucas. His expression seemed impassive, but Lucas suspected he was furious.

"What's going on?" he asked.

Lucas winced, and hurriedly introduced Keach and Amanda. The back door of the squad car opened and a man in a black suit stepped out.

"I'll handle this." He extended a hand to Amanda's front door. "Let's take this inside, shall we?"

"Who are you?" Lucas asked, blocking the man from moving forward.

"Ray Tennif. FBI." The man brushed past Keach and Lucas, strode past Amanda.

"Good morning to you, too," she muttered. Rolling her eyes at Lucas and Keach, she led them inside her office.

Ray Tennif looked around as though hoping he were any place but here. Lucas also checked out the office, which consisted of two small rooms that had desks and chairs, but apart from Amanda, no other occupants.

"I gave my assistant the morning off," she said. "She's getting a root canal."

Ray took a seat in Amanda's swivel chair at the large desk right inside the entrance and pointed to the two chairs opposite him. "You two sit here. Amanda, bring us coffee."

"Sir, yes sir."

Ray squinted at her. "No need to be snarky."

"Whatever you say, douche canoe."

His eyes widened and they both burst out laughing.

The officer who had walked away from the squad car came in with a small plastic bag and handed it to Ray.

"Thanks, Don. Please wait outside." Ray glanced from Lucas to Keach.

Lucas was still trying to get his measure of the FBI agent. One moment he was all business, the next he was laughing. The delicious scent of brewing coffee soothed Lucas's anguish, and he tried to feel better about his decision not to tell Keach what he knew.

"When is somebody going to tell me what's going on?" Keach asked.

Ray glanced toward the other room where Amanda was busy making coffee. "Perhaps we should wait."

Seconds later, she emerged with a laden tray and deposited cups in front of the others. "Grab a chair for me, will ya?" she asked Lucas.

He grabbed one from the other room and brought it over to her desk. She squeezed in beside Keach and Lucas, who were forced to move over.

"Thanks, lucky pants. Now, everyone, help yourself to cream and sugar. I'm not your slave. Ray, why don't you tell Keach the latest. I know that Lucas has been briefed."

Lucas cringed when Keach's head whipped around to him, his gaze affixed to Lucas's left temple.

"Am I in trouble?" Keach seemed confused, and Lucas didn't blame him.

Ray emptied several packs of artificial sweetener into his coffee. "No, Mr. McKennie, you're not. We just need to explain a few things." He leaned back in Amanda's chair and drummed his fingers with a dramatic flair on the armrests. "We found a body on the outskirts of Tahoe. Well, the remains of a body."

"Lucas mentioned that to me. Outside the place my dad used to own."

"Right." Ray shot an accusatory glance at Lucas.

Lucas held up a hand. "That's all I told him."

"Okay." Ray stopped drumming. "We tried for a long time to get DNA samples from your brother, because we were certain the remains belonged to Bella Boston. All we knew was that she was an orphan and there were no known relatives other than your brother."

Keach said nothing, but his posture made him look like he was bracing himself for bad news.

Fuck. I shoulda told him before we came here. Lucas waited for Ray to drop his bomb.

"Bella Boston has been missing without a trace, as you know, for decades. Your father was always a suspect in her disappearance. When we found these bones, we had a forensic pathologist out here from Washington working on another case of a missing woman who's been known as Jane Doe since 1982. Also found in Tahoe. She was the victim of a serial killer, and therefore, we didn't think she was related to the Bella Boston case."

"Why not?" Lucas was curious. His boss hadn't told him this part of the story.

"We got a tip-off about the body found at the old McKennie residence. This body was found after Jane Doe's remains were discovered. Her killer was already incarcerated. Actually, he'd killed himself by the time Bella Boston vanished."

"Okay." Lucas nodded. It was disconcerting to know that there was such devilish work being perpetrated in such a beautiful, remote place.

Ray seemed excited as he went on. "Using very advanced forensic genetic genealogy techniques, our expert made history on these two cases. We haven't made any announcements yet, but the body we found on your father's old property has no genetic tie-in to your brother."

"So it's not Bella Boston?" Keach asked.

"I didn't say that."

Keach's eyes widened. "Wait. What are you saying? I thought you couldn't get my brother to give you DNA."

"We had an informant who removed a used cup from his

house. I'm not saying who, but it turned out to be very useful. We struck out with your brother, but we found strands of hair that didn't belong to the victim. They belonged to the person we believe killed Bella Boston."

"And who was that?" Keach strained forward, anguish etched in his features.

"Through a bit of research, we discovered that the victim and suspect were related. It's actually the first time a victim and perpetrator have been identified with this genetic coding. We were able to do this with the help of the Jane Doe Project in conjunction with GEDmatch, which is a brand-new DNA and genetics database. It's only been in use in law enforcement since last year, and our Jane Doe was the first case used for it."

Ray hardly sat still as he continued. "This program will revolutionize DNA testing and give fresh life to some cold cases going back decades. We were able to identify the two women in the Tahoe cases by backing them up with fingerprints. You see, the suspect in the Bella Boston case had a prior conviction, a misdemeanor for driving a stolen car way back in the late seventies. We had her fingerprints on file."

"Her?" Keach seemed coiled, wound up like a snake.

"Yes, *her*. The killer and victim were sisters." Ray looked right at Keach. "The killer was your mother."

"That's impossible," Keach began, but he froze as the words left his lips. He glanced over at Lucas. His expression was one of sheer and utter shock.

Lucas had hardly believed it himself when his boss had told him. Anything was possible, of course. But this was clearly too much for Keach. He obviously hadn't expected any of this, from all appearances. He fell silent. Ray shot Lucas a glance laced with guilt.

Lucas shifted his gaze, aware of Keach's sagging body posture and Amanda's frank scrutiny.

Ray leaned across the desk toward Keach. "We talked to a few of your mother's old friends. Are you aware she was writing her autobiography? I've read it. What it lacks in, ah, finesse, she sure makes up for it with spicy detail. I still have the manuscript in my office. I can get you a copy of it."

Keach said nothing. He had a bewildered look on his face. At least a minute later, he said, "But what does this mean for my brother? Was Bella his mother or not?"

Ray waited a beat, then responded. "Yes and no. She and your dad adopted him, but she didn't take to motherhood very well. Harper said, in her memoirs, she and Bella were sisters. Your mom always loved your dad, but her parents wouldn't let her date him because she was only fifteen when they met. Your dad had worked on her father's cars, which was how they met. He was infatuated with Harper but kept a respectful distance. She says Bella was a few years older and he married her because she pursued him. Bella and your mom were very competitive, according to her book."

Keach looked incredulous. "I can't believe what I'm hearing. Are you sure they were related?"

"Yep. Your dad fell hard for Bella because she was so beautiful. He was obsessed with her and promised her parents he would always take care of her."

Keach interjected. "Where are her parents? I've never met them."

Ray stared at him. "They died a long time ago. Died in a house fire in Tehachapi. They had fallen out with their daughters by the time Bella disappeared. They always blamed your dad. When your mom married him, they quit talking to her altogether."

"How do you know this?"

"It's in the book. Your mom kept the family secret that Bella was her sister because it would have looked bad if people knew who she was once she married your dad. She also claims she was the real birth mother for your brother Michael."

"Does Michael know?"

Ray shrugged. "We don't know."

"I can't imagine he does. His whole life was based around his mother vanishing. It's been the weight in his heart for so long." Keach paused. "I feel so stupid. I should have guessed Bella and Mom might have been related. The resemblance between my mom and Bella was . . . uncanny. She sandbagged Bella all the time though, so I just thought my dad had a thing for brittle blondes."

Ray nodded. "Apparently, by the time Harper was of legal age, she and Bella both slept with him. The sisters fought over him."

"They fought over my dad?" Keach shook his head. "Women always dug him. I never got it. He was a moody guy and not particularly nice to them."

"Some women like the bad guys," Amanda said.

"Yeah. True." Keach nodded.

"He apparently had a huge dick, which was an attraction," Ray said.

"Good god." Keach looked taken aback. "Don't tell me that's in the book."

"Sure is. Some of the details are lurid, but according to Harper, Bella didn't particularly want a baby, and it was hard for Harper to pretend Michael wasn't her own."

Keach rubbed his face. "She and my brother had a horrible relationship. And all that time, she was his real mother."

"According to her, Bella resented motherhood. She frequently left your brother in public places. A bank one time. A grocery store another. According to Harper, when Michael was a toddler, she once tied him to a lamppost outside a liquor store like he was a dog. Bella forgot about him and left him there. Harper claims she found Bella lying on the front porch of their home doped up on Quaaludes, drinking a bottle of rye. Harper sent your dad to drive around and look for your brother."

"Geez," Keach said. "The sainted Bella's fans would be horrified if they knew this." He ran a hand through his hair. "I never knew any of this. I'll be honest with you. My mom hated Bella. She lived in her shadow, and my dad never let her forget that Bella had been the love of his life. She had a love-hate relationship with my brother."

He looked over at Lucas. "My brother took a year off once to go look for Bella. Not knowing what happened to her almost destroyed him. He once cried when we had a bad storm, and he worried she was stuck somewhere in bad weather. Mike also worried that somebody had her tied up in a basement doing unspeakable things to her. I don't believe he has any clue she wasn't his birth mom."

"Your dad and Bella adopted Michael Jr. in a private arrangement. Nothing on record about who the mother was. Then we got hold of the memoirs, and since then got your brother's DNA from the cup, but we'd like to check yours, too."

"And Mom wrote all about this adoption?"

"Yep."

"How did you come across this memoir?"

Ray looked at Keach in a way that suggested he was trying to formulate an appropriate response. "It was in a safety deposit box at the bank." He seemed to be waiting for Keach to say something.

"I know nothing about that," Keach said.

"I suspected as much. Two people were given keys and permission to access it. Your mom and your brother. They were the joint executors of your father's estate."

"There was an estate?" Keach seemed stunned.

"We began an investigation into your brother's activities

last year. We discovered the presence of the safety deposit box, which we learned had been accessed only by him once your mom passed. The bank was forced to turn over the contents to the FBI when we started the DNA processing of what we believed were Bella's remains last year. Your brother fought to get the rights to whatever was in that box, since your mom made him sole executor of the estate." He paused. "You seem surprised."

"I wasn't speaking to my dad when he died, but my mom always acted like she was broke. I was the one who took her in and cared for her in the last weeks of her life. I paid her medicals bills and fed her. It drove my lover, Joe, crazy having her there. He wasn't, um, very, ah, supportive about it. It put a lot of stress on our relationship, but she was my mom." He blew out a breath. "I certainly didn't know there were any assets, or that my brother had control over them. They must have had a good laugh at my expense."

Ray shook his head. "Maybe. But your brother lost the case. He was never able to get his hands on the money that was left in the safety deposit box, or your mother's memoirs. There were stocks and bonds, certificates of deposits. A lot of investment information in there. Your father left a complicated estate that's still hanging in the wind. All of it under federal protection."

"I never even knew about any of it." Keach looked bewildered. "My mother never let on there was any money. She did tell me she invested in some scheme of my brother's that didn't work out."

"Well, that wasn't true. He's got surfboard shops and other businesses. He's amassed over sixty million dollars."

"That's a lot of surfboards," Lucas muttered.

"What my mom told me sounded very strange, actually," Keach said. "I knew my brother had money, because he bought a ticket in the space program I work for. In fact, he just bought a second one."

Ray seemed shocked. "He did? When?"

"I just found out today, so you can imagine I'm stunned to learn Britty asked him to find someone to kill me."

"I think he's covering his tracks, so in the event you do die, nobody can pin it to him," Lucas said.

"Geez. I hope you're wrong." Keach blew out a sigh. "Mom was pretty distraught over her dealings with Mike. She wouldn't say much to me, but she asked me to help. So I hired a forensic accountant to chase the money. I wasn't informed of the details. All I know is he was never able to find any cash anywhere." He frowned. "And now you tell me there was an actual estate."

"That's interesting," Lucas said. "When I first investigated your brother, I couldn't find much in the way of actual businesses associated with him, or any kind of paper trail."

Ray nodded. "Right. Like most rich men, he's buried his holdings in LLCs and under company names."

"Sounds to me like your mother was somehow involved with all this and wanted you to *think* there was no money," Amanda said.

"I hope you're wrong, but it makes sense," Keach responded.

Lucas caught Keach's attention. "You know, it could be that she and your brother wanted to make sure there was no way to find the money. Which, of course, you didn't. Or your accountant didn't, anyway."

"When you tried to cash that check, you unleashed holy hell," Ray said. "That account your dad had written it on has been red-flagged for over a decade. We were able to find it hidden in some old trust funds he'd created for you and your brother, then dissolved. The funds were diverted elsewhere. We're not sure where, yet."

"Jay-zus." Keach looked ill. "And I'm the one who cared

for Harper right until the end."

"Did your brother ever visit her?" Ray asked.

"Rarely. He FaceTimed her a lot. He sent a gift basket of fruit one time, and the fruit was all rotten when it arrived. He said he'd bought it from some discount food supplier. It was weird."

"You remember the name?" Ray asked.

"No. But I've got it written down in a notebook at home. I couldn't get hold of them to send a replacement."

"You're right. That is weird," Amanda said.

"Wait, I remember now. Bixby Foods. Some place in Carson. Or on a street called Carson. The delivery guy was vague. I was amazed how bad that fruit was but gave up trying to get replacements. I never got an answer to my calls. The line rang and rang. There was no website. Nothing. I just figured my brother didn't give a shit about my mom and wouldn't do anything about replacing the fruit she craved." He closed his eyes for a moment. "At the end, the last few months, I had round-the-clock nursing for her. Mike checked on us with phone calls a few times a week. I was grateful for that, let me tell you. But he never came over.

"By then, all my mom could eat, or *would* eat, was one type of yogurt and pureed pieces of fruit. He came the day she died, and he knew I was distraught. He was the one who made the calls to have the hospital bed and oxygen tanks returned to the hospice that had delivered them. I loved my mother. Damn." His face twisted in grief, and he slid into silence again.

"I'm very sorry for your loss," Amanda said.

He glanced across the table at her and Ray. "Do you have any idea why Thomas English wants me dead? I mean, I really don't know the guy well. And why he would ask my own brother to do it?"

Ray shook his head. "We have whispers and rumors. I can't

elaborate right now."

"Of course not," Keach muttered, his tone bitter. "Mike and Mom kept so many things hidden from me. Can you tell me what she wrote about me?"

Ray squirmed. "Maybe you shouldn't read the book after all."

"Oh, man. That bad, huh?"

Ray picked up the plastic bag on his desk. "If you're willing, I'd like to take some DNA and compare it with your mom's and your brother's."

"To see if we're related?" Keach looked devastated. "What the hell did she say about me? Does she claim I was adopted too?"

Ray hesitated. "No. Look, I'd rather you read it for yourself. When you feel up to it."

Keach's gaze flew to the door.

Is he contemplating running? Lucas felt gutted for the guy. *It can't be easy sitting there, listening to one revelation after another.*

Ray seemed oblivious to Keach's dismay.

"Do you mind if I swab you for DNA?"

Keach tensed up. "My mother gave birth to me. I know that for a fact."

"How do you know that? For a fact?"

"There's video. My dad shot it. A home birth. In a plastic blow-up pool in our old living room. Made me sick watching it. All that blood and my mother wailing." He sank back farther in his seat. "But since I have no idea where the tape is now, if you really need a swab, I'll give it."

Ray seemed way too excited about the task at hand. He took out a vial saying, "Open your mouth for me," and swabbed the inside of Keach's mouth.

Lucas stepped outside to call his boss. "This case is getting creepy," Lucas said as soon as Pringle answered his phone.

"Tell me about it. Listen, Mike McKennie was arrested at his apartment in Reno and somehow eluded the apprehending officers by attacking them with their own Tasers. Don't ask. He's on the loose somewhere up there. His baby mama, Talon Zabransky, was in the apartment, too. She was arrested earlier, but he got her out super-quick. This guy has connections. We had her in custody thanks to an outstanding bench warrant on a DUI charge. There was an error in the paperwork, though, and McKennie was able to get her out. She didn't even have to see a judge. She had to sign papers saying she would return to court when they file the claims against her."

"What about her baby?"

"Child Protective Services in Washoe County has the kid. She had no food or clothes for him, and from what I understand, she deliberately created a distraction so that McKennie managed to escape confinement." He paused. "She said there was no next of kin she trusted with him, but she's got connections, that girl, thanks to McKennie, so although she was apprehended a second time, I don't think she'll be cooling her heels in jail for very long. Once again."

"And what about Keach? Is he still in danger?" Lucas asked.

"Not sure. Thomas English—Britty's bunk got tossed this morning, and they found an illegal cell phone in there. He made one call since Mike visited him, but that was to his attorney, and he hasn't used the prison pay phones to contact anyone. We don't know if Mike pursued the hit. We had him, damn it. Can't believe we lost him."

"Just because Britty didn't reach out to anybody else doesn't mean he didn't find someone else to take on the assignment," Lucas said. "Or that Mike won't follow through."

"True, but we have no proof anything like that happened. We gotta hope Mike McKennie doesn't hate his brother enough to follow through with the hit."

"So Keach still isn't off the hook."

"Right." Pringle sighed. "We're actively looking for Mike McKennie and any known accomplices in several places. Four different police divisions are involved. We even hit Keach McKennie's apartment early this morning, in case somebody was hiding there waiting to attack him. You might wanna tell him his place looks ransacked. There's almost nothing in there."

"I think he did that himself. I mentioned to you his ex-boyfriend, Joe, and how he took a lot of their furnishings. And Keach got rid of some stuff himself." The sudden memory of a bunch of chocolate rolls and other choice junk food in Keach's trunk made him hungry. He'd pop the thing open and grab some for the journey back to LA.

"Okay," Pringle said. "Your friend Keach is having one hell of a shitty day. Head back here. Tennif took some DNA from him, right?"

"Yep. We'll take another car, like we discussed before, unless you want us to fly back."

"Fly back? Let's not go overboard here. We don't even know why Britty ordered the hit on Keach. The guy seems clean. A bit of a weirdo with his tickets to the moon crap, but there's no evidence he's involved with the family business."

"Nope," Lucas said. "He was astonished to hear there was even an estate left by his father and passed on to Mike by Harper McKennie."

"Sounds like your typical dysfunctional family. Anyway, LAPD won't spring for the kind of funds it takes to buy last-minute plane tickets. Just swap out his vehicle and let me know what you pick out."

"Okay, boss."

"And don't call me boss."

Lucas almost smiled. It was something of a running joke between him and Pringle, but he found nothing amusing about Keach's current predicament. He was about to pop the trunk of the Prius when Ray snatched the keys from his fingers.

"Keach tells me this car key is a spare." Ray removed it from Keach's keyring. "He's got another one on him. I'm gonna drive this over to the federal building. It'll be safe there until you get back here to pick it up. We've got you a Bronco for the drive back."

Lucas glanced to where Ray was pointing. Keach and Amanda were circling the vehicle, shaking their heads. "That beat-up old thing?"

"Yeah. Ain't it great? Drives like a dream, but we got it with some dents, so it doesn't look like a cop car. Call me when you make it back to LA."

"Will do." Lucas waved to the uniformed patrol officers as they drove off in the squad car. He made it over to Amanda as Keach took a call on his cell phone.

"Are you making it with him?" Amanda asked, tilting her head toward Keach.

He didn't get a chance to respond. Somebody screamed as an explosion filled the air, and Lucas and Amanda were lifted off their feet. He searched for Keach, who was flying back against a tree. Lucas hit the ground, covering Amanda's body with his own. People came running as glass and metal debris rose in the air.

Lucas rolled over with some effort. He looked over in the direction of Keach's car. Well, where Keach's car used to be. A big black hole had replaced it, and charred remains burned in the eerie silence that followed the detonation.

And then the sirens and choppers came.

Chapter Nine

It was a lot to take in and none of it good. *Who tried to kill me?* Keach kept staring at the mangled remnants of his Prius and realized it could have been Mike, since he'd evaded police custody earlier in the day. *Did he have a tracking device on my car?* Too late to figure that out now. It was awful to think of Ray Tennif being killed. The police reported there were no other casualties unless you counted businesses that sustained damage.

Amanda hugged him, saying, "It could have been you. Glad you're okay." She seemed to sense Keach needed some hand-holding.

In short order, Keach, Lucas, and Amanda were given an armed escort to the police station right by the mall. Two SWAT team officers fired questions at him and Lucas, but everything seemed to be coming at him from a distance.

The watch commander asked him to submit another DNA sample and he complied.

"We'll get you out of here now," Lucas said.

"I feel awful that you're going through this because of me," Keach said.

Lucas held his gaze. "It's not your fault."

"But your overnight bag and your laptop were in the car."

"I have no attachment to clothes." Lucas reached out when nobody was looking and squeezed his hand. "The laptop was an LAPD one. They'll replace it. But I can't replace you, and that's all I care about."

Keach stared at him. For a guy who said he got sick of

people easily, Lucas acted anything but around him. "Do you think Ray has a wife? Kids?"

"I don't think so. But whoever did this just bought themselves a boatload of trouble."

A federal marshal was assigned to Keach and showed up in a vintage Woody. Keach was intrigued by it, and the marshal. Justin Farber was a good-looking, dark-haired man who wore the kind of *casual* clothes he imagined marshals wore off duty. He'd been fishing with his sons on a rare day off but seemed unfazed by the interruption.

"I moved to Reno to get away from bombs and other explosives," Farber said. "Who knew?" Along with crisp blue jeans and a checked shirt, he wore a fanny pack that might have held innocent objects, but Keach figured it included a gun.

In fact, when Farber escorted him and Lucas to the airport, he was forced to reveal what was inside the fanny pack, and there were two guns. They were just in time to take a Jet Blue flight to Long Beach. Passengers in the front row were disgruntled when they were forced to move to accommodate them.

Farber ignored the irate stares, then spent most of the flight reading something on a small electronic notebook as he sat beside Keach. He waved away any refreshments offered by the flight attendant. Lucas glowered at them from across the aisle as he drank bottled water and accepted the free snacks. Not that Keach cared. His stomach was in knots. He hadn't called his insurance company yet, and all the new stuff he'd bought had burned up with his car.

Now I have to start again. And oh, God. That poor man was killed. He'd asked the cops around him if Ray was married. Did he have kids? Would they miss him? Lucas had said he didn't think he had a wife or any offspring. He felt relieved when Farber told him Ray had been divorced and there were no kids.

Keach couldn't let go of the thought that Ray could have been a father with small kids left without him. *Did my father ever think about the risks he was taking with his apparent life of crime when I was a kid?* He closed his eyes and day-dreamed for the duration of the eighty-minute flight. He kept trying to imagine being naked with Lucas, but he kept seeing Ray getting into the Prius.

Then . . .

Boom!

As the plane landed, waves of anxiety swept over Keach.

For the first time, Farber spoke to him once the seatbelt sign had been turned off. "You've had quite the adventure, Mr. McKennie."

"Please, call me Keach."

"Keach. You stick close to me and don't make eye contact with anybody." He tilted his head toward Lucas. "Except him."

They were allowed off the plane, which disembarked right on the tarmac. Keach was surprised to see a squad car waiting for them at the hastily assembled steps. Ground crew looked up at them as Keach and the others walked down. He realized everything he had was in the Prius. His clothes and cell phone. He'd left it in the charger. *I feel like I am coming back into my body. I can't decide whether to run or sleep for a thousand years.*

He glanced over his shoulder at Lucas, who was already on his phone and frowning as they reached the squad car.

"I've been deputized as a US Marshal, sir," Lucas said into his phone. "This is still my case, and I will stay with Keach until the end." He jabbed a digit on the phone and climbed into the car with Keach and Farber.

"They told me you were a pushy guy," Farber said with a smile.

Sandwiched between Lucas and Farber, Keach asked, "Where are we going?"

"You'll see." Farber was making calls on his own phone.

The squad car drove away from the airplane toward the exit. When Keach looked back, he noticed the plane's other occupants were still on board. Several blocks away, the squad car stopped. The officer at the wheel turned around.

"We're here, sir."

"Good. Thanks. Come on, Keach. Lucas, stay behind him."

They all got out and headed down a laneway that had seen better days. At the end, a white sedan waited for them. Keach blinked as the driver nodded at Farber.

Once again, he found himself sandwiched in the backseat between Lucas and Farber. The tension in the vehicle was so thick, Keach thought he'd suffocate.

"Can we open a window, please?" he asked.

"Put on the AC instead," Farber barked. He had an app opened on his electronic notebook that seemed to be a street map. "No problems so far."

They rode in silence until they approached a circular blue sign with a backdrop of a bucolic beach setting saying, *Bixby Knolls."*

"Bixby! That's the name—"

Farber put a finger to his lips before Keach could finish his sentence. They arrived at a small apartment building on a street called Carson.

Keach leaned forward as they paused and then kept moving along the street of what looked like empty houses. He gazed at Farber, who shook his head.

The whole area seemed dilapidated and . . . abandoned.

Farber was tapping something into his cell phone when, at the end of another street, the driver said, "Which way, sir?"

"Haven't you been told?"

"No." The driver turned to look over his shoulder at Farber, a fearful look in his eyes. His cell phone rang. "That might be the team leader now."

"Answer it." Farber's tone was terse. A black car rolled up

beside them, and Farber's cell phone pinged. "Never mind."

Farber gestured to Lucas, who opened the door. Once again, Keach joined Lucas and Farber as they got out of one car and got into another.

Keach longed for explanations but thought he might be sick. The vehicle took off, and several minutes later they were entering a neighborhood called Wrigley. Again, they drove down a street that contained what looked like empty homes.

What the hell is going on?

Farber kept working on his notebook and his cell phone as they drove around. Twice more they rolled through strange areas, including one spooky section of the tough West Adams neighborhood. It seemed industrial yet abandoned, the downtown high rises visible in the distance. They seemed like silent witnesses to whatever was really going on in the neighborhood.

They reached a sub-division called West Athens. Keach had never heard of some of the suburbs they passed. Again, there were houses lining streets that looked empty.

"What gives?" Keach asked.

"I'll explain," Farber said. He instructed the driver to pull over. "This is fine, right here. Thanks."

The driver seemed surprised as he loitered at the curb. "Are you sure?"

Farber frowned. "Of course, I'm sure." He opened the back door, stepped out, and indicated for Keach and Lucas to follow him. He leaned inside the vehicle. "Thanks. You can go now." He waited for the driver to merge with the sparse traffic again. "Wait," he instructed Keach and Lucas.

As soon as the car had turned the next corner, Farber beckoned them to follow as he crossed the road. They walked a few blocks, switching sides often.

"What are you worried about? Us being followed?" Lucas asked as he and Keach trotted to keep pace with the guy.

"Nah, I'm just having a bit of fun seeing you two

scrambling to keep up with me." He suddenly grabbed Keach's arm. "Get down. Both of you!"

He dragged Keach down onto some dried-out grassy patch in somebody's front yard. Lucas threw himself beside them.

Keach glanced up in time to see a vehicle driving slowly along the street.

"That was the car that just dropped us off," Lucas whispered.

"Yes. Which is why I got rid of the driver." Farber sat up. "We'll get out of here, but now we're here, you may as well check it out."

"But we're being followed," Keach protested.

"Oh, no. He's not following us. *He's* being followed. Somebody knows you're back in LA, which means your brother has some excellent police sources." Farber opened his electronic notebook. "Our driver did a good job of leading them on a wild goose chase. LAPD will take over any minute now and stop the vehicle that's been trailing us for the last six miles." He stuck out his bottom lip and stared at Keach. "None of this is familiar to you, I can tell."

Farber stood and extended a hand to Keach, who took it. He, in turn, helped Lucas rise.

"I smell dog poop," Keach said. "Hope I didn't sit in it."

"Nah," Lucas said. "I stepped in it." He busied himself with scraping his shoe against the dried-out grass.

Farber checked his cell phone as it pinged. "Good. Nobody followed us." He glanced at Keach. "I know you both lost your belongings in the explosion. By the time we get to the safe house, one of our agents will have basic replacements for you, courtesy of our victims' fund." He gave them a wan smile. "I'll explain about the merry-go-round we just took. What you just saw was the result of your brother's investments. All those empty houses and old declining neighborhoods." He shook his head. "He's made a career of buying places nobody else is willing to pay for."

"As what?" Lucas asked. "Shady business dealings?"

"You got it. Fake businesses, such as the fruit company that brought Keach's mother rotten fruit. We know about that. We've been watching Mike McKennie for a long time. Most of his dealings involved Thomas English and his family. I suspect Britty felt Keach blew the lid off their operation by trying to cash that check. He—and Mike—had no idea how close we'd come to arresting them anyway. Trying to kill you and then taking out a federal agent sealed their fate. We have enough on Britty to put him away for life. Now we just have to find Mike."

A car pulled up, a big, black Escalade that easily accommodated them all in the back. The driver handed them chilled bottles of water. Keach guzzled his, feeling much better for it.

"You don't need to stay with Keach," Farber told Lucas.

"Oh, I'm staying. I'll square it away with my boss." His eyes glittered in fury when he said, "Keach needs all the protection he can get. Somehow, even with officers posted outside Amanda's office, somebody managed to plant a bomb on his car."

"We don't know when the bomb was planted on the car. Could have happened when you were at the motel. Or at breakfast. Somebody had to be close enough to activate the timer, I'll give you that, but the crime scene is still being investigated. The officers who were outside Amanda's office didn't see anything."

"Right." Lucas's voice dripped with fury. "Besides, I've been deputized as a marshal, thanks to another case. I have every right to protect him."

Farber said nothing but tapped away into his cell phone then his electronic notebook. "Done," he said finally.

"Can you tell us more about the houses Mike bought?" Keach asked.

Farber glanced away from him. "Everything that went in and out of these houses involved stolen classic cars hidden in garages, modified, then smuggled to big-ticket buyers. They smuggled drugs and weapons to distributors across the country hidden in car parts. It was quite clever, actually, until Britty's brother got involved and blabbed to the wrong person."

"I think we saw him up in Tahoe," Keach said.

"Not a huge surprise. We know he was up there spring cleaning a couple of drop houses they have up there," Farber responded.

"We saw piled-up garbage bags around one property," Lucas said.

"Yeah. We picked them up. Mostly take-out remnants and empty Amazon packaging."

"Amazon packaging?" Lucas asked.

"That's how people buy guns now. Online. They buy parts and put them all together. The whole weapons thing is changing. Fast. We know Britty was in charge of operations in Reno and other parts of Nevada. He has a cousin operating out of Las Vegas, another in Laughlin."

"Laughlin?" Lucas asked. "Who the hell buys property out there?"

Farber pointed at him. "Exactly. The ATF confiscated over a hundred thousand weapons from two homes in Reno and unboxed parts in Laughlin. All of them had been shipped from properties we just drove by."

"And my brother's involved in this?" Keach was incredulous.

"Your brother's involved financially. He ponies up the funds and collects high rewards. He's got money to burn." Farber unleashed a weird, feral grin. "That's why he bought two tickets to Mars from you. He really thinks it's a way to escape."

"He does? I thought he was just trying to provide an alibi for himself, that if he was buying tickets from me, he couldn't be orchestrating my homicide."

"We're interested in learning where they've moved their operations to. They've been rapidly clearing out each house since Britty got jailed a month ago." Farber shot Keach a glance. "You walked into one hell of a mess."

"If Britty's brother blabbed, why's he still alive? Why do they want to kill me?" Keach asked.

"Because he's useful. He's the clean-up guy."

"Oh. I see. And I'm not."

"Right."

Keach tried to ignore the pangs of anxiety scratching away at his psyche. *Mike would never kill me. Would he?* Lucas and Farber were talking about the weapons that Mike was shifting around the country. Keach listened, his head spinning with each new revelation from Farber.

"The ATF has been watching Mike. He and his crew had been purchasing multiple gun parts online and putting them together. Anyone can do it with access to a YouTube video."

"That's frightening to know," Lucas murmured.

"Of course, it is. We have our work cut out for us." Farber's tone turned angry. "People think the sporting goods stores selling weapons are the big problem. They're not. It's all gone underground, and to be frank, we can't keep up with it."

Keach kept an eye on the passing scenery as they veered into Hollywood. There were tour buses everywhere, and he glimpsed a group of people dressed as Spider-man, Super-man, and Wonder Woman, posing for photos with tourists on Hollywood Boulevard.

As the driver edged along a street called Laurel, Keach felt uneasy. He wanted to check they weren't being followed and turned.

"It's okay," Farber assured him. "We're in the clear."

A few minutes later they rolled up Nichols Canyon to a house on a long, winding street called West Granito Drive. Keach instantly understood why the location was good. Only one side of the road had housing. The other was nothing but flat scrub and a sheer drop into the canyon. The house itself was surrounded by cypress trees.

The driver pulled into the driveway, and once again, Keach, Lucas, and Farber were on the move. They headed down toward the back of the property and entered the house from the kitchen door. Inside, the place was a hive of activity with cops in uniform and what Keach assumed were federal agents milling about watching several monitors.

"What's up?" Farber asked.

"No idea where McKennie is," one of the uniformed officers said. "He's been dormant since seven AM."

"That's weird," Farber responded. "He's normally like Chatty Cathy on that damned cell phone of his."

"He might have junked it," one of the officers said. "Our informant slipped off the radar for a couple of hours. He just made contact. Says he hasn't seen McKennie but had to lay low because the entire operation is falling apart. People are being sacked left and right. We may have to pull him out soon. He says McKennie doesn't trust anyone."

"I'm not surprised, since he's such a lowlife himself." Farber shot a glance at Keach. "Sorry."

"Don't apologize to me. I couldn't agree with you more."

Farber focused his attention on Keach and Lucas. "There are some clean clothes in the bedrooms. Why don't you guys take a shower? We've got food coming. It's just sandwiches, but . . ."

"I adore sandwiches," Lucas said.

Keach and Lucas went to their rooms, Keach stomping down on all his fantasies of shower sex with Lucas. He grabbed the towel and soap on his bed and picked up the new clothes and headed to his bathroom. The window had a corner view of the street. The neighborhood was quiet, and no cars were circling the vicinity, so why was he nervous?

His teeth almost chattered as he cleaned up. The shower was refreshing. He turned off the taps but held his breath when a shadowy figure appeared at the frosted glass bathtub door. Somebody thrust it open.

Lucas. He stood there, fresh and clean, in a shirt and pants. He laughed at Keach. "What, you thought I was your brother?" He frowned and must have realized how nervous Keach was. "You really think I'm gonna let anyone touch you?"

Keach stayed quiet until the screech of tires outside had him jumping three feet into the air.

"Shit," Lucas said and peered out of the window.

Keach almost fell out of the tub in his haste to look. A black car, with black tinted windows, drove past the house. Bullets rang from the windows.

"Holy crap!" Keach shouted as Lucas ran from the bathroom.

A uniformed officer came in looking for Keach. "Get dressed," he ordered, ignoring Keach's nakedness. Then he gave Keach a harsh look. "Put some clothes on, for fuck's sake." Out of nowhere, he pulled out a gun. There was a lot of commotion in the house and more bullets being fired.

"You're not a cop," Keach said, frozen in terror.

"You're a lot smarter than your brother said. Now. Get. Dressed."

Keach complied, too frightened to dry off. His skin was wet as he re-dressed.

"You are one lucky son of a gun," the fake cop said.

Keach recognized him now as one of the two cops who'd been outside Amanda's office. "You followed us down here?" he asked, incredulous.

"Drove like maniacs. Lost you for a while. Then we found you. It's easy to infiltrate a house loaded with cops when you're dressed like one."

"But we flew here," Keach said. He put the lid down and sat on the toilet, about to don the socks and shoes he'd been given.

"I was on the same flight, moron." The fake cop struck him hard in the head. He'd hit Keach's ear, and blood trickled down his face. "Stop wasting time. Your brother doesn't care if you're wearing shoes or if you're barefoot. Get moving."

Keach wavered on the seat. Another blow sent him to the floor. He closed his eyes, hoping the beating would stop. He suddenly saw his father's face in his mind's eye.

"Don't keep schtum!" his father shouted.

Keach was aware of the fake cop bending over him. It took everything in him to reach up and punch the guy. The fake cop fell back. Keach screamed. "Lucas!"

The fake cop hit the tiled floor, and Keach grabbed the nearest weapon he could find. Shaving foam. He sprayed it into the fake cop's face, then punched the guy in the head. The fake cop had the gun trained on him, but Keach jerked it away. A shot rang out, hitting the shower faucet. Another shot—this time it hit glass, because the shattering sound and the shards hitting Keach woke him up. He wrestled the gun away from the fake cop by biting his hand.

The guy screamed, and Keach kicked him in the face.

They grappled on the floor until Lucas and Farber came running. It was Farber who put a bullet in the guy's shoulder while Lucas ran to Keach.

"We got your brother. Damn. He's out front." He took Keach's face in his hands. "You hear me? We got him!"

"This is it. Make yourself at home."

"Did you just move in or something? Your place looks

134

empty." Keach thought he would never, ever be able to relax again, even though Lucas's West LA pad was cool, quiet, and inviting. Every sound made him jump, and the doctor had told him the head blows he'd suffered had left him with a broken eardrum.

He would know in a couple of weeks if he'd require surgery. He still didn't know why his brother had gone to such lengths to kill him except that he told the police he blamed Keach for screwing up his life.

There were a lot of things that needed to be settled now. It had been a shock to learn his beloved Robert, and even Joe, had been involved in the *family* business.

Keach hadn't even been able to talk to them. Or Michael. Yet. It was a big case with many parts and sad pieces to it. Keach knew he was the son of his father and mother. He didn't need DNA to prove it. In the end, his father had come to him, across time and death, to save him.

His father. Not his mother.

Lucas touched Keach's face, bringing him back to the present. "I like open spaces. I bet you'll want to furnish every room here by the end of the weekend."

"Not necessarily. I emptied my own place, remember?"

"Yeah, but babe, I saw the trunk full of stuff you bought. Pots, pans, clothes. Food. You like stuff. And that's okay. I'll let you furnish. But no doilies and no floral cushions. Please."

Keach didn't know how to respond. Was Lucas really saying they had a future? *Wait. Do I look like a guy who's into doilies?*

Lucas went to the kitchen and opened the fridge. He was peering into it as Keach followed him. "I have peanut butter and bread. I make a mean peanut butter sandwich. Want one?"

Keach smiled. "You forgot to shop?"

"No, sir. I never shop until I need more peanut butter. Look." He opened a kitchen cabinet that was stuffed with jars of the stuff.

"I'll pass, thanks," Keach said.

"What, you don't trust my cuisine?"

"It's not that. I still feel crappy. My stomach's in knots."

"I can understand that. This hasn't been fun, but there's always the need for a good peanut butter sandwich. It fixes everything, I tell you."

"If you say so."

"I do say so. Besides, the feds promised us sandwiches. They never gave them to us."

"True."

"Come on, you should have something to eat. I can make coffee, too."

"Man cannot live by peanut butter sandwiches alone." Keach couldn't stop grinning at the guy.

"That's my motto in life." Lucas made the sandwiches and switched on his Keurig. He leaned into Keach for a kiss as they waited for the coffee to drip into their cups. They took their food out to the living room, which had a couple of plants, a sofa, a small coffee table, and two wing chairs. Nothing else. Lucas pushed open a balcony door and announced, "We have a table and chairs outside."

"No." Keach didn't want anyone taking potshots at him again.

Lucas put his coffee and sandwich on the coffee table and swiftly moved over to him. He took Keach's face in his hands. "Nobody's going to hurt you ever again. If you let me, I can take care of you. Your brother's not getting out anytime soon, and you're off the hook. Everybody knows you weren't involved in his business."

"I still can't believe that he talked Robert and Joe into working with him."

Lucas shrugged and reached for a sandwich. "It was easy, fast money. They probably never thought you'd find that check."

"Right." Keach shook his head as he sat beside Lucas on the sofa and bit into the sandwich. "You're right. This is good."

Lucas lay back on the sofa and seemed to fall asleep, even after having had a cup of coffee.

Keach was restless. He got up and checked that the front door was locked, then walked around from room to room. His thoughts tumbled as he wandered around the place. Lucas had a calming home with a lot less clutter than most people. It seemed shocking that the guy chose to live like this all the time. He half-feared spotting a sleek black car passing by the windows but kept telling himself to chill. *Calm down.* It wasn't easy.

"Where are you?" Lucas called out. "Everything okay in there?"

Keach returned to the living room. "I'm fine." He rolled his eyes when he noticed that Lucas, who was still stretched out on the sofa, was watching a mixed martial arts match. He glanced down at Lucas, but he seemed fixated with the young Asian woman who was beating another woman to a pulp. Her hapless victim didn't even look like a woman, she was so masculine.

"Why do you like this stuff?" he asked, wedging himself beside Lucas at the end of the sofa. He picked up Lucas's bare feet and put them on his lap.

"I like underdogs. I also like the fact this girl wasn't supposed to win but did." Lucas turned his head and smiled at Keach. "I also like people who can take care of themselves. Like you."

Keach couldn't help grinning.

Lucas turned off the TV. "You may end up inheriting a lot of money when all is said and done. Do you realize that?"

"I don't want it. I mean, who doesn't want a windfall? But

hell. Nothing's worse than knowing your family is a bunch of thieves and killers."

"Yeah, but babe, money is money. You could do a lot of good with it."

"Maybe." *Will I ever feel safe again?* Going back to his place hadn't been an option. Lucas had insisted on bringing him here. *But what about tomorrow? And the next day? And the day after that?*

He knew he still had to go back to the West LA precinct to answer a bunch of questions in the morning, but he had other mountains to climb at the moment. He reached over Lucas's feet and started rubbing his cock through his jeans. Lucas was rigid, straining against the confines of his tight pants.

"You need help," Keach murmured.

"Clearly," Lucas said. He laughed and moved his hands down to his zipper.

Keach batted it away. "Stop that."

Lucas shook his head but showed infinite patience as Keach finally undid the zipper and worked on removing everything.

"Slow down," Lucas whispered.

"Nuh-uh. If I learned anything today, it was never waste a moment having a good time.

"Let me introduce you to my bedroom, then," Lucas said. "Argrggh," he yelled as Keach dropped to his knees.

He lapped at Lucas's leaking cock, slowly sucking in Lucas's shaft, wishing they had all the time in the world. He swayed a little, thanks to his ear injury, and reached out to hold on to something.

Lucas held him, pulling Keach up to him, kissing him hard. He lifted Keach to his feet. It all happened so fast. They practically tore off each other's clothes and clashed with tongues, lips, and fingers aiming for faces, necks, and cocks straining for attention.

"You okay, babe?" Lucas asked, his voice gentle.

"I'm doing great. I'm enjoying this." Keach returned his attention to Lucas's cock. He knelt once more and ran his tongue around the width of it, capturing the head again. He gently wrapped his fingers around Lucas's weighty ball sac, keeping him exactly where he wanted him.

Lucas groaned when Keach's lips smacked the base of his cock. He looked down to watch as Keach lavished him with kisses and tongue, pleasure mixed with surprise etched in his gaze.

"Fuck," he whispered, throwing his head back for a moment.

Keach kept sucking, playing with his own cock. He was so turned on he couldn't see straight.

Lucas reached down, easing Keach away from his meaty shaft. He gazed at Keach's cock, helped him up again, kissed him, then led him to the bedroom.

Keach didn't have too much time to take in the bare surroundings. Lucas pushed him playfully way onto the bed, his face wreathed in smiles as he hunkered beside him, licking and sucking his way down Keach's body. He moved his hand over to hold onto Keach's cock. Keach let out a yelp of pleasure as Lucas moved between his legs, forcing them open.

"Damn. Rubbers are in the bathroom." He got up and ran, cock bouncing in the air.

"Are you kidding me?" Keach raised himself on one elbow. "In all those gay romance novels I read, the guys always miraculously have rubbers and lube in their nightstand drawers."

Lucas laughed as he returned with a couple of square foil packages. "These are pre-lubed. Now, where were we?"

They resumed where he'd left off. They got all worked up again, and Lucas gloved up, using his sheathed cock to stroke Keach's asshole.

"Oh, my God," Keach ground out. "Oh, I'm gonna come!"

Lucas entered him, and Keach flailed on the bed. He pulled Lucas closer as he fucked him hard and deep. Keach saw stars. Oh, yeah. Lucas was good. Lucas let out a wild moan.

Keach looked up at him as Lucas, sweat glazing his face, returned his gaze.

"I have a confession to make," Lucas said, his voice hoarse. He was still inside Keach, his cock slowly moving in and out of him. He bent down and kissed Keach's face.

"What's that?" Keach asked.

"I'll never get sick of you. I want to be with you. Rich or poor."

"I love you," Keach said.

"I love you, too." Lucas looked surprised. He blew out a breath. "Just one thing though. Can you ever get used to peanut butter sandwiches? I mean, a lot of them?"

"Hell, yeah." Keach laughed, then reached up and grabbed Lucas's head. "Just watch me try."

You may also enjoy the following from eXtasy Books Inc:

Blood Eclipse
A.J. Llewellyn and D.J. Manly

Excerpt

Rezoning laws had recently made room for vampire brothels in this neighborhood as well as the other fetish clubs.

Now they were moving on up north to Hollywood. Beyond the hills and into the San Fernando Valley would come next, he was certain. Rory felt dismayed as they crossed the cobblestoned courtyard. He had to admit the vamps had restored the crumbling, old, mock castle into pristine condition. As they approached the wide oak front door, Rory could hear music, some tune he sort of knew the words to. He froze suddenly.

"What?" Dennis said. His face was flushed with excitement. "You look great, don't worry."

Rory felt dizzy. Looking great was not what he was worried about. He recognized this crazy pop song as the signature tune Kolin Karolyi played walking to the ring the night Libreto died. He played it for each of his fights. Rory felt his throat tightening. He couldn't be here . . . no.

"Let me see," Dennis said, grabbing his arm and pulling

him aside.

Rory was grateful for the delay.

Dennis ruffled Rory's blond hair, which hit his collar, curling a little. He placed his hands on his broad shoulders, nodding in approval at Rory's choice of a silky navy shirt and decently snug, faded designer jeans. "Now, if I was as cute as you, I wouldn't have anything to worry about. And don't worry about money, I'm taking care of everything. Let loose and have a good time."

"What am I supposed to do when you're . . . you know?" Rory sucked in some breath.

"There are other mortals here, like us. Make friends, dance, get laid." He grinned, slapping him on the back.

Rory shook his head. "You know, Dennis, you're perfectly good looking. I wish you'd stop saying that I'm cuter than you. We could leave this place, go into WeHo and you could pick up a—"

"Don't back out on me now. This is what I want. Okay?"

Rory nodded. "Okay."

Two muscular bouncers with electronic bugs fitted into their ears checked their names on a portable handheld monitor. Granted access, the heavy door swung open unaided. Rory admired the remnant of the old Magic Castle. They walked down the dark corridor and his eyes adjusted to the light. It was still a den of red velvet and gaudy gilt fixtures, but there was a decided Goth stamp to everything. A room to the left still featured the image of a Victorian female ghost playing a piano. Her image flickered on and off and at times, the piano appeared to play itself.

Rory had butterflies in his stomach when he glimpsed a counter with an unattended coat check and another door right beside it. Kolin Karolyi, who was more bulked out since Rory last saw him, stood in front of the door, arms akimbo. The door opened as if by magic and the song changed to a sultry blues number and Rory could hear whistling and hooting. He trembled.

He took a breath, told himself everything would be all right.

"Hi," Dennis grinned at Kolin Karolyi, not realizing who he was. "Is this where we pay?"

Karolyi, who had obviously become overly friendly with roids, looked as if he could double for the Frankenstein monster. He flicked a glance at Rory but showed no sign of recognition. He nodded curtly. "Fifty-dollar cover, there are no tables left."

"I made a reservation," he said, which surprised Rory. "Name's Dennis Cotton."

"When did you do that?" Rory asked in a low voice as Dennis handed the doorman some money.

"A few days ago," Dennis said absently, focused on the transaction.

"A few days ago? Then everything was an act. You would have come here anyway — without me?"

"I knew you'd give in eventually," he grinned at him. "Don't be mad."

Rory muttered under his breath as the doorman asked, "Are you looking to rent sexual entertainment?"

"I am," Dennis said. "Not him," he hooked his thumb toward Rory.

"Okay," he said, "follow me. I take you to your table and then you need check in with the regulator. It's the booth near the bar."

Rory narrowed his eyes, keeping close to Dennis' heels as they entered the main part of the club. He had to walk rather quickly, weaving in and out of a crowd of boisterous men who were dancing and drinking and ogling the stripper on the huge elevated stage in the front.

All around them, the music pumped like an accelerated heartbeat, throbbing with sexual heat. When they arrived at their table near the front, Rory's gaze was riveted to the naked dancer who slithered across the stage like a seductive serpent, his eyes glowing with some preternatural light, his beauty actually creating some kind of unholy glow around his perfectly sculptured body.

It was Dennis who grabbed his arm and pushed him down into a chair, grinning like a kid who had just been presented with a shiny new toy. "Sit," he said. "I have to go see the regulator and get my sheet."

"Sheet?" Rory muttered, trying to tear his gaze away from the hypnotism going on in front of him. "What sheet?"

"All these hunks have numbers. I have to reserve if I want one and hopefully I'll get the one I choose. Demand exceeds supply in these places. Thank God these vamps can do one mortal after another. Order drinks. I'll be back."

A half-naked Asian was standing in front of Rory suddenly, holding a tray. Beautiful but then they were all beautiful, weren't they? "Not all of us," he said. "What can I get for you, sweetie?"

The waiter was leaning down next to him, his face close to his. Rory instinctively moved his head away. "Ah, two rum and Cokes, I guess. And did you just read my thoughts?"

The waiter grinned and winked at him, walking off without a word, presumably in the direction of the bar. Rory couldn't see anything through the crowd, not even where Dennis had gone.

The table he was at was small, only big enough for two, and right beside him was a larger table filled with six young men who were talking loudly and chugging beer. One of them reached up to touch the dancer on the stage, but he moved out of reach so fast, Rory saw only a flash. The dancer hissed, his fangs coming into view and that, too, seemed to last only a heartbeat. Then his expression became unreadable.

Rory was plummeted back to the past and a memory buried by grief. Damn. He needed his computer. He remembered he'd packed his mini portable screen pad and withdrew it from his pocket and scribbled away with his stylus.

I went to Panama City three weeks before the fight to watch

Barrera train. His trainer, with whom he was living in virtual seclusion, treated us to lunch at an outdoor cafe on the beach. I ordered the house special, a Panamanian favorite of smoked tuna dip. I was delighted when it came with fried bow-tie pasta for dipping.

Barrera eyed my meal enviously. He could not have anything fried. He had to stick to a diet of soups and salads to hit his target fight weight. He ordered sancocho, a local specialty. It was a stew and when I took a bite, he asked me what I thought was in it. I said, "Vegetables, a nice broth but the chicken is kinda stringy."

He laughed and said, "It's peacock. The poor-man's chicken." I felt grief stricken to have consumed such a lovely, colorful bird. Barrera laughed and said, "Mi amigo, you ate a small bite. Me, I eat it all. I take the consequences . . . not you."

The consequences. For the second time that day, Rory thought on those exact words. He felt a bad storm coming . . . he just didn't know from where.

About the Author

A.J. Llewellyn is a multi-published author of over 300 M/M erotic romantic novels who was born in Australia, and lives in Los Angeles. An early obsession with Robinson Crusoe led to a lifelong love affair with islands, particularly Hawaii and Easter Island.

Being marooned once on Wedding Cake Island in Australia cured her of a passion for fishing, but led to a plotline for a novel. A.J.'s friends live in fear because even the smallest details of their lives usually wind up in her stories. A.J. has a desire to paint, draw, juggle, work for the FBI, walk a tightrope with an elephant, be a chess champion, a steeplejack, master chef, and a world-class surfer. She can't do any of these things, so she writes about them instead.

A.J. started life as a journalist and boxing columnist, and still enjoys interrogating, er, interviewing people to find out what makes them tick.

How to find/friend me:

email: ajllewellyn@gmail.com
website: www.ajllewellyn.com
www.facebook.com/aj.llewellyn
www.twitter.com/ajllewellyn

Newsletter sign-up:
ajllewellynnewsletter@gmail.com
– each month I give away a free ebook!

D.J. Manly

I write not only for my own pleasure, but for the pleasure of my readers. I can't remember a time in my life when I haven't written and told stories. When I'm not writing, I'm dreaming about writing. Eroticism between consenting adults, in all its many forms is the icing on the cake of life but one does not live by sex alone. The story of how two people find love in spite of the odds is what really turns me on.

Find D.J. Online:
E-mail: armandmanior@yahoo.com
Facebook: https://www.facebook.com/dante.manly
Twitter: https://www.twitter.com/djnovels
Website: http://djmanlynovels.simplesite.com

www.ingramcontent.com/pod-product-compliance
Lightning Source LLC
Chambersburg PA
CBHW070749120626
46557CB00002B/511